ONE LAST BITE

LEAH CUPPS

INKUBATOR
BOOKS

Published by Inkubator Books
www.inkubatorbooks.com

ISBN (eBook): 978-1-83756-368-5
ISBN (Paperback): 978-1-83756-369-2
ISBN (Hardback): 978-1-83756-370-8

PROLOGUE

I peer across the restaurant, my eyes catching on the glint of handcuffs.

If those don't end up on my wrists by the end of the day, I'll be damn lucky.

It isn't the first time the police have been called out to the barn-turned-restaurant, and it probably won't be the last. The dining room we're sitting in is normally full of wealthy diners eager to taste the famed fare. But now? It's the backdrop for about a dozen police officers. I sigh.

It was good while it lasted.

I return my attention to the carefully folded linen napkin in front of me. Fumbling with the corners, I try to focus on the words coming out of my mouth.

Slow, deliberate, and above all—*vague.*

"Ma'am?" The detective rights himself in the chair across from me, trying to get my attention. "When did you say you found the blood?"

"About two hours ago." My voice shakes, belying the shock that has taken over my body.

"Hmm." He raises a crusty eyebrow at me, surely questioning my response. The serious tone in his voice and the deep wrinkles in his forehead make me shift in my seat. "Why did you wait to call us?"

I breathe in to steady myself. As I inhale, I can still smell the hint of baked bread floating in from the kitchen. Hundreds of loaves have been baked here over the years. The smell of the dough rising seems to cling to the air. I make a mental note to grab the yeast starter from the kitchen. I mean, why waste it?

"Ma'am?"

Oh, right, crusty eyebrows is waiting.

"The cell phone service is dodgy at best, and the electricity ran out when the storm hit last night." The words are coming out faster than I intend. I'm afraid if I start talking and tell my story, I won't be able to stop. "Needless to say, it wasn't easy to make the call."

Thistle, the restaurant we're sitting in, is located in the heart of Maine, about five miles from the nearest highway and even farther from the nearest town. The power out here can be patchy, especially on an old farm. The glittering chandeliers above us flicker as if on cue, fading in and out from the tenuous power supply. *Bon Appétit* labeled it "barn chic." I almost smile, thinking back to the time we stood in the kitchen, leaning over the magazine. Our faces and our beautiful restaurant leaping off the pages in front of us. It was a perfect night. One of the best we've had here. One of the few good ones.

Almost as a reflex, the inspector taps his phone. I can see from my seat across the table he has barely a bar left. He nods and says nothing. Another officer pads past us, holding his phone up in the air to search for a signal.

See, I'm not lying. *Yet.*

"Was anyone else present when you found the body?"

The question turns my stomach. One person. But that person is long gone by now, probably miles down the interstate.

"No," I reply. My voice sounds convincing, even to me.

The boards behind me creak and groan. I hear more footsteps. The floors have a life of their own, the sounds they make a comforting chorus of old hickory. Though they are old, worn and stained, they're still beautiful. If those planks could talk, oh, the stories they would tell. I almost want to reach out and touch them, say goodbye to a beloved part of the barn.

A young, lanky police officer walks up to our table, his lips pursed and his eyebrows drawn together. I can feel the cold air floating off his skin.

I know where he's been. And I'm pretty sure I know what he's found.

"Detective, you need to see this." He swallows; his face turns a shade more pale. "It's in the freezer."

PART I

SADIE

1

THREE MONTHS EARLIER

N*orah Winthrop.*

I stare at her. Blunt, chocolate-colored bob. Sharp green eyes. She wears a black button-down shirt with a clean starched collar. She's just like the photos I've seen of her in magazines, every inch pristine and manicured.

I shift in my seat, fumbling with a squirrelly lock of hair that has fallen into my eyes. Norah and I couldn't be more opposite. I'm sure she can barely stand the sight of my thrift-store khakis and white tee shirt. But these clothes are the best I have, and they're clean. The campground I've been living in doesn't exactly have an ironing board on hand.

The words that ran across my mind when I stepped through the front door pop up again.

There is no way I am getting this job.

I still can't believe I'm sitting here. The beams above me hold sparkling chandeliers that have cast their light over celebrities, politicians, and the who's who of the upper East Coast. This restaurant basically put destination dining on the map. Sitting for an interview is definitely the closest I'm going to get to the dining room here.

A few years ago, Norah and her husband, Devon, owned and operated one of the hottest restaurants in New York, Pepper. The name was a bit meta for my taste, but it gave the swanky eatery an artistic flair that the upper class craved. I remember reading the article pronouncing Pepper the new *it* spot in New York. It was a glowing review, fat with praise of the monkfish stew and creamy lemon risotto.

I had been standing in the magazine aisle in Barnes & Noble when I saw her for the first time. Her nary-a-strand-out-of-place hair contrasted sharply with her fair skin and pale green eyes. Devon was next to her—tan, tall, and much more relaxed. They made a striking couple.

I sat down with the magazine at a table and ordered a small cappuccino I could barely afford. The menu for Pepper had been carefully photographed and laid across two pages; I pored over each glossy photo, tracing the words with my fingers.

Smoked salmon with green pea risotto and asparagus foam. Mussels with celery and chili. Foie gras parfait with green beans, grain mustard, and almonds. Every ingredient on the menu felt like a carefully selected collection of jewels set out on display.

After the coffee cup was empty and the last few readers had left the store, I still sat there in awe. I was so inspired by her work. I couldn't bear the thought of putting the magazine back on the shelf, so I slid the magazine under my arm and stepped away into the bathroom. Hiding in a stall, I took out my sharpest chef's knife and cleanly sliced four pages from the magazine, stashing them in my bag. I dropped the magazine carcass back on the stand where I'd found it as I slipped out the door.

When I arrived back at my matchbox-sized apartment, I carefully pinned the pages to the wall, where they stayed for the next three years.

Unfortunately, about six months ago, I had to leave them behind along with everything else.

"Sadie, it says here you were a sous chef at Château Bernard?"

It's all I can do to keep from biting my fingernails, which are now practically whittled down to the nubs. It's a horrible habit, one I've been trying to kick for years.

"Yes, for one year."

Her green eyes shift, narrowing in on me. Heat rises under my cheeks.

"So you know Chef François?"

I smooth the pleats of my khaki pants, trying to push the sweat off my palms. "I do. But primarily I worked under Peter, he was second in charge."

I point my fingers toward the cheaply printed résumé she's holding, hoping she doesn't notice my chewed-off nails.

"I've included his number, there."

"I see." Norah nods and pulls the paper closer to her face. "Well, I look forward to speaking with Peter."

I swallow hard, trying not to flinch at the thought of her talking to Peter about me. I've held up my end of the bargain, but now that I'm far away, will he still keep up his end? I told him I have pictures of him cheating on me with François's wife, which was a bit of a white lie. Even if I had those photos, I have no way to send them to François now. If Peter calls my bluff, he could say anything about me. He knew me intimately, after all.

I smooth my features, but Norah is squinting at my résumé.

"You went to the Culinary Institute of America?"

"Yes," I say as my stomach turns. "But I wasn't able to finish."

At least I'm being honest about that.

"Oh, and why is that?"

I clear my throat. "I couldn't afford the tuition."

Norah gives me an empty stare. She is an intimidating woman despite her slight size. I often wonder how a successful chef stays in shape despite creating decadent sauces and roasting rich meats on a daily basis. Perhaps she's one of *those* women with a swirling metabolism who devours calories and churns them out in a puff of smoke.

Me? I'm not so lucky. I frequently taste the goods I am preparing, and as a result, I keep a few more curves on my body than I would like. In fact, I feel downright frumpy in front of this sophisticated culinary icon, starched collar and all.

I straighten my posture, remembering something my dad told me about faking it till you make it.

"But I've been saving money so I can go back and finish in a couple of years."

"I see."

Norah suddenly straightens her back against the metal-framed bistro chair. It creaks in response. "Well, Sadie, I have to say, your résumé fits the bill. Of course, I need to make a few calls, but..." She pauses, looking me in the eyes. "I think we may have something for you here. When would you be able to start?"

I can feel the neurons firing in my brain, trying to make

their way down to my lips. I open my mouth and close it. *Wait...is she offering me a job?*

"Sadie?"

She has to be kidding, right?

"Anytime." I sit up in my seat, knocking the table setting in front of me in several different directions. I quickly put the fork, napkin, and plate back in their places. "I mean, I'm available to start as soon as you need me."

Norah leans back, touching her earlobe as she looks me up and down. "Wonderful. I'll call you very soon." She slides her chair back to stand.

"Sounds perfect," I say as I leap to my feet and extend my hand to her, practically vibrating from head to toe.

As Norah extends her hand in return, I notice a few spots on her arm. I think at first it's maybe a birthmark, but the coloring is a dark blue. Like a bruise. I've seen these types of marks before; the pattern resembles the grip of a hand. She seems to notice my gaze on her arm and quickly pulls away.

"Norah, we need you!" I hear a voice shouting from the kitchen behind her.

"Until then," she says, giving me one final once-over before turning her back on me.

I open my mouth to speak, but she's already gone.

2

You might need to lower your expectations.

That's what Sally Henshaw told me on my first day at Mike's Diner. It was right after I asked her where the table linens were located.

The greasy roadside stop isn't exactly where I thought I'd be when I turned twenty-two years old. A one-story long rectangle with a few sagging boards on the outside and about twenty layers of paint inside. When diners pull open the front door, a tiny bell rings and a greasy breeze rolls out to them.

Mike's Diner wasn't exactly my first choice of kitchen jobs, but it's been just over a week since I sat across from Norah in the dining room at Thistle. And so far I've heard exactly nothing. No email, no phone call, and most definitely no offer for a job. I left a few messages with the hostess, a stone-cold woman who practically hung up on me as soon as she heard my voice. At this point, she probably thinks I'm stalking Norah. The last time I called, she suggested I give Norah some time and be patient so as not to bother her anymore. Basically, she told me not to call again.

"Sadie!" Mike hollers from across the small kitchen. "Table five is ready for their order."

Right.

Mike's pays what little bills I have, and at the very least, I'm cooking every day. The only catch? I have to wait tables too.

"Now!" His deep voice booms across the kitchen. I know better than to ignore his calls. A memory of his six-foot-three and three-hundred-pound frame squeezing into the kitchen to retrieve me this morning gets me hustling to the table.

"Coming!"

I smooth a sweaty curl from my cheek and brush it behind my ear. The chicken-fried steak is still popping from its grease bath as I slide it onto the plate. I've created a nest of mashed potatoes that holds it securely in place as I spoon gravy over the top. I reach into the metal bin on the shelf above my head to pull a few sprigs of parsley and place them carefully.

I hear a few heavy steps approaching from behind me. The smell of overapplied drugstore perfume tickles my nose. I don't even have to look around to see who's standing behind me.

"It's beautiful," Sally says, touching my shoulder. "But you know Joe the semitruck delivery driver doesn't give a damn what his chicken-fried steak looks like, right?"

My shoulders fall. She's right. But it feels wrong to throw everything in a giant heap and dump it on the plate. Surely the cow who died for this meal deserves a more dignified delivery.

"I suppose you're right," I say, looking at the presentation.

“Where’d you get the green stuff?”

“I bought it at a roadside stand.”

“Oh, Sadie.” Sally pats me on the shoulder.

Sally, despite her husky voice and sleeve of tattoos, has a heart of gold. When I showed up here a few months ago desperate for work, she gave me the job even though I was very overqualified. We even shared a drink together after one particularly crazy shift, and I actually told her the real story about my past. She’s the silver lining to an otherwise dire situation.

“What the heck is going on here?” I hear Mike’s gruff voice behind me. “This is a truck stop, not a fine dining restaurant, dammit! Get your head out of your ass and feed my customers, now!”

I straighten my back and feel my cheeks burn. “Sorry, Mike!”

I grab the plate and head for the kitchen door. I can’t afford to lose this job, even if I’ll only be here for another week.

The tips are fairly crappy, and the grease-filled diner is not what I imagined when I studied at culinary school, but it puts money in my pocket and also allows me to afford my car insurance and save for school.

I place my back against the swinging kitchen door and push my way out into the diner.

Mike’s isn’t going to make the hot list in *Food* magazine any time soon, but man, is it busy. Truck drivers, cops, EMTs rolling off an eighteen-hour shift—they all crowd into the twenty-table diner to enjoy a hot meal.

“Well, shoot, look at this. It’s a thing of beauty,” Joe says as I lay his food in front of him. He grabs the plate and hoists it up in the air. "Look at what this little sweet tart made for me, fellas. Seems like she might want to spend some time in the bunk of my semi cab later!"

With this, he takes his finger and thrusts it in and out of the mashed potatoes.

The whole diner erupts in laughter. I freeze in my spot for a few seconds, cheeks burning and tears stinging my eyes. Joe turns his face back toward me, but before he can say another word, I turn and hustle back toward the kitchen.

When I'm safely out of sight, I take a deep breath and try to regain my composure. At least no one slapped me on the butt on my way back to the kitchen. But the day is still young.

I have got to get out of here.

I spent years at CIA mastering sauces, developing the perfect stock, and refining my palate. All that was thrown out the window when I humbly accepted the job at Mike's. Here, I don't cook steaks' temperature to order. They're served on a white porcelain plate, chicken-fried to perfection, with a side of canned gravy. When I first started here, I felt like a culinary angel fallen from the sky.

Then again, I was never an angel to begin with.

But my job here is temporary. Mike's niece, Rebecca, was on maternity leave when I got the job. Rebecca is a longtime employee of the diner. Everyone loves her, from the kitchen to the front door. She has regulars, fans of her cooking and her sassy one-liners.

I am her temporary replacement. My work ethic has earned the respect of everyone at the diner except for Mike himself, who never seems to be satisfied with anything I do. As much as Sally says Mike wants to keep me, they just can't afford two cooks. I don't blame him; Rebecca is his niece, after all.

So my days here are numbered. Seven days, to be exact. Part of me is elated at the idea of leaving this grease stack behind. The other part of me is wondering what the heck I'm going to do for money. If I lose my car, I'll be left with a tent, some clothes, and a few culinary school books. I will be officially homeless.

When I didn't hear back from Norah, I started interviewing at other places. Pretty much anywhere within a one-hundred-mile radius that's looking to hire a cook for their kitchen. The options are slim, but I want to stay close to Thistle just in case something opens up.

I tighten the strings on my apron and get back to work. It's not like I want to stay here forever anyway, but with both my parents gone, I don't have a ton of options. Which reminds me, it's been a few hours since I checked my phone.

I brush past the stainless-steel sink to the small storage room in the back where I've hidden my purse behind a few sacks of flour. I pull out my phone and see several missed calls and texts. My pulse quickens with anticipation. Maybe I'll get some good news for once.

The first message is from a small barbeque restaurant about twenty miles down the highway. I wipe the grease from my cheek and press the phone against my ear.

"Hi, Sadie, this is Derek from Bubba Buck's Belly Busting Barbecue. Unfortunately, we have decided to go with another—"

I don't even listen to the rest of the message before hitting delete. My heart sinks deeper into my stomach.

The sounds of chatter and plates on steel grow louder

outside the storage room door. I close it until the latch clicks so I can listen to the next message.

"Hello, Sadie, this is Norah Winthrop. Please give me a call back at your earliest convenience."

My heartbeat picks back up. *Finally!*

I twist the lock on the door and dial the number she left on my voicemail. After four rings, she picks up.

"This is Norah."

"Hi, Norah, this is Sadie Jackson. You left me a voicemail about the kitchen position?"

"Oh yes, Sadie," she says. I can hear the clattering of pans in the background. "Let me step outside. Hold on for just a moment."

"Sure," I say. My palms are sweating now, mixing with the grease from the kitchen, causing the phone to slide in my grip. I wait in silence for a few moments.

"Would you be available to start on Monday?"

I'm speechless for a moment. *This is really happening.*

"Monday would be great!" My voice sounds high-pitched. I'm trying not to come across as desperate, but my heart is pounding in my ears.

"Great. Can you be here at ten a.m.?"

My mind is reeling as I imagine myself working in Norah's famous kitchen. To see the monkfish stew prepared in front of my eyes. I'll be able to see precisely what seasonings she uses, how the stock is prepared...

"Sadie, are you there?"

"Yes, I'm here. That sounds perfect," I say, recovering myself. "I'll see you Monday."

"Goodbye."

She hangs up on me before I'm able to utter a response. I hear banging on the door behind me.

"Sadie! Table six is waiting for their order!"

I take a deep breath and stash my phone away in my purse. Norah Winthrop has just hired me for a job.

And she doesn't even know what I've done.

3

I roll down the window on my beat-up Honda Civic as the wheels crunch over the gravel driveway. The road to the restaurant winds its way like a snake to the front door. I try to focus on the sweet smell of lavender and honeysuckle floating in through my open window, instead of the sweat pooling under my arms.

The Winthrop estate is stunning. Apple trees line a long drive, and a matching row of black picket fence posts are lined up to salute guests as they enter. Wildflower blossoms rub shoulders with the manicured hedges, and it all feels organic yet planned at the same time. I've never been to England, but I imagine this is what it would look like.

Even though it's a cool sixty degrees in Maine, I'm sweating in my car. Did I put on deodorant this morning? Apparently I didn't use enough, because the sweat rings are growing under my arms. I feel a bit like an imposter, unworthy of the whole Winthrop experience.

Regardless of how I feel, I'm here. After I park my car, I sit with my hands at ten and two on the steering wheel.

Deep breath, Sadie. You got this.

My plan here is simple. First and foremost, stay employed long enough to add *cook at Thistle* to my résumé. If I can manage that, I'll be able to get an executive chef position at a lesser-known restaurant.

This will also give me time to save up and return to culinary school. Norah didn't really give me an idea of what she'd be paying me, but given how little my expenses are, it should be enough to get by. Once I finish my degree from CIA, it's only a matter of time and maybe a little luck before I find an investor willing to back the restaurant I've been dreaming of opening since I was ten.

The sound of shouting on the far side of the barn catches my attention and drags me out of my head. I peer through the windshield. It's Norah herself, wearing a tee shirt and slacks with a white apron tucked around her waist. The man she's talking to is dressed in the same way. He has wavy dark hair and olive skin.

My window is down, and I can almost make out a few words. I turn my head slightly so I don't make eye contact.

"What do you mean it's not about the money?" I hear her say. "It's always about the money! You should know that by now. If we don't pay them back, we're dead! All of us."

Norah is waving her hands as she yells. From what I've read, Norah can be pretty dramatic, and now I see that's true. I can't hear what the man standing with her is saying, but he places his hands on her shoulders. She relaxes slightly. He's speaking in a low tone.

After a few minutes, I see Norah throw up her hands and storm off toward one of the cabins. As she does, the man turns and catches sight of me in my car.

Oh no, I hope he doesn't think I was listening. It's my first day, and the last thing I want to do is act like I'm snooping.

Without missing a beat, he raises his hand to wave and makes his way toward my car. I pop open the door and step out to greet him.

Here goes nothing.

"Hi, I'm Sadie," I say, reaching out my hand. "Norah hired me to—"

"*Hola*, Sadie," he says, taking my hand in his. His hands are slightly calloused. He has a strong grip and a slight accent. "Norah told me you were coming. My name is Luis. I'm the sous chef here at Thistle. Please come with me."

Luis is...not what I expected. He has broad shoulders, a slight tan, and caramel eyes. He's not quite six feet tall, but he carries himself with the confidence of a much larger man. The confidence doesn't surprise me, given that he runs a large kitchen staff in a well-known restaurant.

I follow his lead, heading toward the restaurant. I steal a glance in the direction Norah left, but I don't see her. From everything I've read, even some threads on Reddit, Norah can be a bit moody as well. I make a mental note to steer clear of her when she's in a mood like today. The last thing I need is to get on her bad side right off the bat.

"So, where are you from?" Luis asks.

"Illinois," I stutter. It's not a complete lie.

"That's a long way from Maine," he says as we step along the paved pathway. I nod in response, not sure what to say. I can practically feel beads of sweat popping up on my nose.

"What about you? Where are you from?" I ask as we approach the barn.

"Me? Guatemala, actually. Even farther than Illinois," he says with a wide grin. His smile is warm and genuine, making an unexpected feeling flutter in my stomach. "So, how much do you know about Thistle?"

"Just what I read on the website," I say.

"Right. Well, the estate is about one hundred acres, with more than a dozen buildings on the property. The restaurant itself is set up in an old bank barn here." He gestures toward the large barn, which is beautifully restored. "Beyond the barn is a small lake with a half dozen cabins around the perimeter. Some of them have been restored, and some are still under construction. Our hope is to offer a boutique-style hotel experience in the future."

I enjoy listening to the rhythm of his voice as we walk. He seems so passionate about this place. As we make our way around the back of the restaurant, he gestures to the large gardens and a large glass building.

"We are known for our farm-to-table cuisine, and this is where many of our ingredients come from. Right in our backyard." He turns to smile at me as we make our way to the back door. "We have several acres of gardens that we harvest three seasons of the year, and in the winter we have a large greenhouse."

"It's amazing," I say, truly in awe of the place. "So, how long have you worked with Norah and Devon?"

"A long time," he says, turning his face away from me for a moment. There's something about the way he says it that makes me think there's a deeper story there. I'm about to ask him a few more questions when he stops in front of a large wooden door with an iron handle. We seem to be at the back of the restaurant.

"Well, here we are. It's probably a bit more rustic than what you're used to, but I promise you the food is fantastic."

Clearly he doesn't know about Mike's.

As Luis swings open the door, I catch my breath. The kitchen of Thistle is an eclectic mixture of modern fixtures and rustic touches. There are four massive stainless-steel workstations that float in the middle of the room, while the walls around the outside are stacked with high-end appliances and equipment. Two rustic posts hold up the center of the room, disclosing the fact that we're standing in an old barn. But there is nothing old about the space.

There are about two cooks per station, with about eight people bustling around the room, working with different specialties. I never made it past the dining room during my interview with Norah, so this is the first time I've seen inside the kitchen. I'm not disappointed.

And the smell. *Wow.* It's a combination of bread baking in the oven, fresh herbs, and garlic. I inhale deeply.

I can feel Luis watching me as I take in the space, probably waiting for me to comment.

"It's really nice," is all I can muster. He nods, smiling, then gestures for me to follow him as we walk farther into the room. We pass a couple of cooks working on food prep. Everything from edible flowers to fresh pork is being chopped, prepped, and stored for the dinner service.

"You can hang up your bag here," he says, pointing to a few lockers posted by the back door. I release the bag from my shoulder and hang it up.

"Now, if you want to follow me, I'll show you around the space," Luis says as he places a light hand on my back. "As today is a Monday, the operations here are pretty relaxed. Thistle only serves diners Thursday through Saturday. Today, we test recipes; we prep the things that need to be slow roasted, the bone broths that need to stew overnight, that sort of thing. It's an easy day to get you started, so you're trained up by the weekend."

He walks me around the space, pointing out each station and piece of equipment with enthusiasm. Most of the appliances I'm familiar with, but it's the first time I've seen someone use liquid nitrogen to make ice cream. My heart beats a little faster as I think about all the new skills I'll pick up while I'm working here.

"You've done a wonderful job," I say.

"Oh, it wasn't just me." He smiles, a gleam in his eye. "This was Norah's vision. She brought this space to life."

"So, where would you like me to start? Norah said—"

He stops in front of a large window that looks over the back of the property. Underneath is a large sink and a mountain of dishes.

"Right here."

I feel my cheeks burn in embarrassment. *Wait, what? Dishwasher?*

I don't have much time to recover because everyone has paused their work and is looking at me. You could hear a pin drop in the room.

"Attention, everyone, this is Sadie, our new dishwasher," Luis says, gesturing in my direction.

"Hi," I squeak. I pull my hand up for an awkward wave. A few of the employees nod and then go back to work.

Luis furrows his brows at me. "Norah didn't tell you that you'd be working as a dishwasher?"

"Oh, no. I mean, yes, of course," I say.

Suddenly my neck, cheeks, and ears become impossibly hot. Of course she wouldn't hire me as a cook in her kitchen; how could I have been so stupid? I'm not even really qualified to work here. It's just, Norah made it sound like I would be cooking.

But I guess she didn't really detail my position when we spoke on the phone. She just asked me when I could start, and I told her. Now I feel like an idiot for getting my hopes up.

It's not that I'm ungrateful, but if only I could show them what I can do. I step in front of the sink and flip on the water.

"I'll get started right away."

"*Bueno*. I'll leave you to it," Luis says and heads to the back door.

I pump a few drops of soap into the sink as the water runs down over the pans. *You're never too good for any job in the kitchen, Skittles, even dishes.*

It's the voice of my father. Skittles was his nickname for me when I was a kid. And he was right—I'm not too good for any job in the kitchen, especially this one.

I eye my messenger bag with my chef's knives hanging by the door. It took me a couple of months of tips from Château Bernard to pay for the set. I was so excited the day I purchased them. I ran to the grocery store and bought practically every kind of vegetable, fruit, and protein I could find. I probably spend three hours slicing and chopping while Iron Chef America played in the background. A few weeks later I purchased a special sharpener to keep them in tip-top shape. I am diligent about sharpening my knives.

I guess they'll have to stay freshly sharpened for another day.

In the meantime, I tell myself I'll wash the dishes to pristine cleanliness until the right opportunity shows up.

I just need one chance.

"Hello, everyone," a cheerful voice booms from the back door. I turn to see Devon Winthrop breeze into the room. I recognize him from the magazine spread in *Taste*. He looks taller in person, well over six feet. He's wearing jeans, a white V-neck tee shirt, and a blazer that fits snugly against his shoulders.

As he approaches my station, I can smell fresh mint on his breath and a hint of cologne.

"You must be Sadie," he says, extending his hand. "I'm Devon Winthrop."

I scramble to wipe my hand off on my apron before offering it to him. His eyes sparkle slightly as he wraps his hand around mine. His grip is soft enough to not crush my fingers, but firm enough to let me know he's in charge.

"Nice to meet you, Mr. Winthrop. Thank you for the opportunity to work here," I say. To be honest, I am a bit starstruck. Not only is he very handsome, he's also the most famous restaurateur I've ever met. I don't know if I've ever actually swooned over someone I just met, but my knees feel like jelly.

"Please, call me Devon," he says, the corners of his mouth curling into a smile. Just as I let go of his hand, Norah appears behind him. Her cheeks are slightly flushed.

"Devon, I need to speak with you, *now*," she says. She glances in my direction with narrowing eyes, but doesn't address me by name.

Devon whirls around to face her, taking a step back. "Norah, darling, I missed you." He leans in to kiss her. Norah quickly turns her head so his lips land on her cheek.

Wow, that was cold.

"Sure, me too," she says, turning her mouth into a tight smile. "Can we talk outside?"

"Of course." Devon turns back to me. "Nice to meet you, Sadie."

"You too," I reply.

Norah has already turned her back on me and is walking to the door. Devon follows behind her.

I turn my attention back to the sink full of burnt pans and crusty dishes. It's going to take me hours to get through the pile in front of me, not to mention the pans currently on the stove. At least I have a view of the property via the large window in front of me.

Devon and Norah are walking toward one of the cabins. They definitely don't seem to be getting along. I can't hear what they're saying exactly, but their body language tells me everything I need to know. They're arguing.

It's really none of my business. My only purpose here is to save up enough money to go back to school and, of course, add Thistle to my résumé.

Besides, I've worked in enough kitchens to know that eventually the gossip always makes its way to the dishwasher. Everyone likes to share their dirty little secrets.

I just won't be sharing mine.

4

I stare at the wrinkles on my fingertips for a moment as I stand over the sink. My back is aching, my feet are swollen, and there are cracks forming in the creases of my hands. It's only my second day of backbreaking work, cleaning and scrubbing every pot, pan, and dish in the kitchen. Not to mention mopping floors and wiping down counters.

As it turns out, my job here in the kitchen isn't just to wash the dishes, but to clean the entire space. I'm basically a glorified janitor.

But even though it feels like only a small step up from Mike's Diner, I'm still working in one of the most famous restaurants in the country. And the pay is much better here.

So there's that.

I try to lean up against the sink to push the kinks out of my lower back.

"Sadie? Have you seen a stainless-steel pot with a copper handle?"

I drop my hands back into the sink and turn to see Devon at my back.

"Oh, hi, Devon," I say, slightly breathless. It's the first time he's spoken to me since yesterday. As a dishwasher, my interaction with the staff has been pretty minimal. "Yes, let me see if I can find it."

Devon watches me as I search through the stacks of pans in front of me and in the cabinet below. He's dressed in his usual dark jeans, white collared shirt, and sport coat. I can smell a faint hint of cologne.

"Here!" I hand him the pot.

"Thank you," he says as he places it on the counter behind him. "I trust you're enjoying your work here at Thistle?"

I rub my dishpan-wrinkled hands together.

"It's been great," I say.

"Hmm." He keeps his deep blue eyes trained on mine. "And how have you been sleeping?"

"Sleeping?"

"Yes." He looks over my shoulder and out the window toward the parking lot. "I noticed you have a blanket and pillow in the back seat of your car."

My cheeks flush. "Well, I—"

I've been sleeping in my car since I started working here, and it's beginning to take a toll on my body. My short stay at the campground has ended. My car is warmer than the thin nylon tent, so it didn't make sense to pay the campsite fee.

Every night after work, I've been driving a couple of miles down the road to find a quiet place to park where no one will see me. I have a blanket and a pillow at least, and I've been able to curl up in the back seat of the car to get a few hours of sleep. Most of the time, sleep eludes me, so I use the light from my phone to reread a frayed copy of *The Flavor Bible* or *Ratio*, books that are widely accepted by chefs to be the gold standard of flavor.

The real trick is sneaking into the employee bathroom early enough in the morning so no one sees me brushing my teeth and attempting to control the curls of my hair. I plan on sneaking into the campsite down the road at least one night a week so I can shower.

"Are we not paying you enough to afford a place to stay?"

I swallow the last bit of saliva. I have no idea what to say in this moment other than to apologize.

"Yes, of course. It's just I've been trying to save as much money as I can. So I can go back to school." I wipe the dishwater off on my apron. My cheeks burn. "I'm sorry, this is so embarrassing."

He waves his hand at me.

"Don't be embarrassed. We've all struggled."

I nod. My stomach is doing flips. I knew I should have hidden my bedding in the trunk. I just didn't think anyone would care enough to snoop around my car. Devon straightens his jacket and shifts his weight, keeping his eyes trained on me.

"Listen, I have an idea. One of the cabins on the lake is partially renovated. It's nothing fancy—a small kitchen, bathroom, and a bedroom. Would you be interested in renting it from us?"

"Oh wow, Devon, that's very generous of you. But I..."

My tongue gets tied up as I try to find the right words.

"But what?"

"Nothing," I say. His eyes look so earnest. I can't say no. "Are you sure?"

"Yes," he says as he strokes his chin. "I tell you what,

since you're trying to save money for school, what if I allow you to stay there in exchange for an extra day of work in the kitchen? Would that work for you?"

"That would be wonderful." My voice sounds a little more desperate than I intend. It's a great offer. Even though I'm already working six days a week, what's one more? I pop a vertebra in my back.

At this point, I'd do anything for a proper bed.

"Great, I'll have Luis bring you a key later today." He points his chin toward the dishes. "Now, it looks like you have a lot of work ahead of you today."

Devon leaves the copper-handled pot on the counter and walks away to one of the other stations. I'm temporarily frozen as I watch him go. This whole situation is turning out better than I imagined. Even if my hands have turned into shriveled prunes.

I return to my sink full of pans and dishes with a renewed sense of determination. I was willing to sleep in my car for as long as it takes to work here, but this is an unexpected bonus. I can literally feel the knots in my neck muscles begin to dissipate just at the thought of a flat bed.

Luis suddenly appears in the kitchen, his musical voice floating into the room. It's clear from the way the staff smile as he enters that everyone loves him. I've caught him on a few occasions gently tutoring a few of the cooks. He never raises his voice and always delivers criticism with a smile.

I try to look busy as he walks toward me, holding two empty baskets.

"*Hola*, Sadie," he says as a lock of auburn hair falls over his forehead.

"Good morning." I nod in return.

"I'm on my way out to the gardens to pick some fresh

produce for dinner tomorrow. Care to join me?" He holds up one of the wooden baskets in his hands.

"Oh wow, yes, I'd love to."

I grab a dish towel and quickly dry my hands as he leads me into the garden. Yesterday, Luis gave me a brief tour of the gardens. And by tour, I mean that he pointed in the general direction of the massive, manicured space, and I salivated over the idea of fresh tomatoes, basil, and anything else that might be growing there.

Part of the charm of Thistle that brings in diners from all of the states is the fact that the ingredients of the food are local...so local, in fact, that they lie just a few hundred feet from the back door of the kitchen.

"Here we are," Luis says triumphantly as we reach the garden. The garden is about an acre, filled with rows of carefully manicured plants, leaves waving in the wind. Luis walks me up and down the rows, pointing out radishes, carrots, potatoes, many other plants, and finally the strawberries.

These are just like the ones I ate as a child. I grew up in a kitchen, and my father often brought me the local produce to savor, like juicy strawberries in the heat of summer. But because we were a diner, not a high-end restaurant, most of our produce was bought at the local food wholesaler or canned. I can remember distinctly the day he brought in the blanched, almost white strawberries from the food delivery truck.

I snagged one of the strawberries from the top of the pile and popped it into my mouth. I'm not sure which was more shocked—my taste buds or my brain.

"Dad, what is this?" I said, holding up the carcass of a sour strawberry.

"Well, that's a strawberry of course," he said with a wry twist of his mouth.

"What's wrong with it?"

Dad chuckled. "Well, our local supplier was sold out. So we had these shipped in from our food wholesaler."

"It tastes horrible!"

He came over and patted me on the head. "Well, Skittles, someday when you're the lead chef of your own restaurant, you'll have first pick of all the good produce."

I remember a warm feeling spreading across my belly. Dad and I had a dream that one day I would have my very own place. I would be the head chef of a classy farm-to-table restaurant, just like the one I'm working in now.

I take a deep breath, inhaling the scent from the lavender bushes that flank the gravel pathway to the garden. For now, I'm just a dishwasher.

Luis must have noticed I'm practically drooling.

"Would you like to try some?"

I blush. "Do you mind?"

"Please," he says, gesturing to the plant. I reach out and pluck a few bright big strawberries from the plant. As I pop the first one in my mouth, it practically bursts, the juices splattering down my chin.

"Oh!" I say, blushing.

"Here, let me help you," he says, pulling a handkerchief from his pocket. I take it gratefully, and we make eye contact for a moment.

I didn't really notice it before, but Luis is *cute.* Not in a chiseled, cowboy sort of way, but he has warm almond eyes that sort of sparkle in the light.

"Luis!"

I turn on my heel to see Norah bounding toward us from the south side of the garden.

"Where have you been? I've been looking for you. I need the appetizer list now, or Devon is going to murder me."

Any warmth that Norah showed me during our interview and on the phone afterward is gone. She's barely spoken a word to me since I started here. She doesn't even acknowledge me as I stand next to Luis.

"Calm down, Norah," Luis says gently. "I've got the list on my desk. Sadie and I were just pulling some fresh herbs and strawberries from the garden."

Norah seems to suddenly become aware of my presence and turns a steely gaze in my direction. I notice a small gold locket hanging around her neck, which I recognize from the magazine photo I saw of her.

"Are you eating strawberries? You know you are not allowed to—"

Luis holds up his hand to stop Norah from continuing. "It was my idea, Norah. Please."

Norah continues to glare at me. "I'd better never see you eating from the garden again. Or else you'll be asked to leave. Is that clear?"

I straighten my back. "I'm so sorry. Yes, I understand."

Norah looks back at Luis. "Let's go."

She begins to stomp back in the direction of the barn. Luis gives me a small shrug and mouths the word *sorry.*

I stand there for a moment, watching them walk back to the barn. One minute Norah is offering me a job. The next moment she nearly fires me for eating a few strawberries from the garden. My shoulders slump. Even though Norah is living my dream life, she definitely isn't the happy and fulfilled person I thought she was going to be.

I guess it's true what they say, *never meet your heroes.*

5

"So what do you think?" asks Luis.

Truthfully? I'm speechless.

The cabin is small, but large enough to hold a kitchenette with a dining table, and a living room. The vaulted ceiling makes it look larger, along with the white-washed wood. On the left side of the room is a kitchen that runs the full length of the space. Cabinets, a small stainless-steel fridge, and a full-size Viking range with a large hood fill the space. There's even a small espresso machine in the corner.

I instantly walk toward the kitchen sink and touch the silver faucet. It's been years since I had my own space with a kitchen to cook in. I want to rip open the cabinet doors and drawers and see if there are plates and utensils, but I resist, feeling Luis's eyes on me.

"It's fully stocked, if that's what you're wondering," he says as a small smile turns the corner of his mouth.

Norah briefly mentioned the cabin is still under construction and in her words "not ready for guests," but this place is nicer than most of the hotel rooms I've stayed in. The faint smell of fresh paint still hangs in the air.

"I think it's perfect," I whisper.

"Let me show you your room," he says, gesturing to the right side of the space, toward a white door. We step into the bedroom, which is set up with fresh white linens, a vintage wooden nightstand, and a small closet. Another door leads to the bathroom, which has a toilet, vanity sink, and claw-foot bathtub with a brushed nickel showerhead.

"The bathroom was finished last week, but there's an issue with the toilet. Devon says we have a new one on order. So you'll need to use the toilet in the main kitchen."

Oh, now I see. I process this. So I need to walk fifty yards to the kitchen every time I need to use the bathroom? It's not incredibly convenient, but I'll take it over sleeping in my car any day.

"No problem," I say.

"I'll leave you to it, then." Luis drops the keys on the kitchen counter. "Good night."

"Good night," I say, still raking my eyes over every detail. "And thank you!" I call after he softly closes the door behind him.

I still can't believe the Winthrops are letting me stay here. After the strawberry incident earlier today, when Norah almost fired me on the spot, I was certain they would recant the offer.

But just as I was finishing up my work for the day, Luis showed up at my side with the keys to the cabin. To say I was relieved is an understatement. If they're willing to give me a cabin to stay in, perhaps that means I have some job security as well.

I walk over to the kitchen and open the vintage-style

refrigerator. To my surprise, there are a few staples inside—milk, eggs, butter, cheese, and some fresh herbs. I pull open the rest of the cabinets to find them stocked with flour, olive oil, and a few spices, plus pots and pans. It's like the kitchen is begging me to break it in.

Even though I'm exhausted from a long day, I find myself throwing together an omelet for dinner. It's been weeks since I touched a sauté pan, and I can feel the joy of cooking down in my toes.

After I clear the last crumb from the plate, I pull my small suitcase out of my car and roll it inside. It only takes a few minutes to stow away my clothes and toiletries in the small dresser in the corner of the bedroom. And of course, I bring in my stack of frayed recipe books and drop them on the kitchen table. The sun has already set, and the light in the room is fading quickly.

I lie down on top of the cheerfully embroidered bedspread, and before I even have time to brush my teeth, I'm asleep.

"Dad!"

I sit straight up in bed, startled for a moment in my surroundings. Sweat clings to my skin and pours down my face. I take a few deep breaths.

It was another nightmare. The room is completely black save for a small pool of moonlight that comes through the window. My shoulders relax, and I remember I'm inside the cabin on the Winthrop estate.

The nightmare is one that has plagued me since the fire. I shudder to think about that night. I was so young. I tried to save what I could, a cookbook that belonged to my mother, a necklace my father had given me. But most of it went up in flames.

There was life before that fire, and then after. Like a deep canyon separating two parts of my life. Dad is gone, but I would give anything for him to be here right now, offering his calming words of comfort.

But he isn't here. As I sit up in my new bed, still on top of the coverlet, I realize my bladder is full. I throw my legs over the side of the bed and walk toward the bathroom. As soon as I pull open the door and see the toilet, I remember.

The toilet isn't working yet.

I sigh. Time for a late-night walk to the bathroom. I take a few strides across the small cabin living room and reach for the front door. I turn the knob.

The door seems to be stuck. I turn the knob again, jiggle the handle. I even throw my weight up against the door. It doesn't budge. I try the key Luis gave me, but it doesn't seem to work.

Great.

Half asleep and still in need of the toilet, I make my way to the window. I flip the latch, tug on the window sash. To my relief, the window opens. It's small, but I'm able to wedge myself into the opening. After a few pushes, I fall onto the freshly mulched landscaping outside the cabin with a small thud.

I quickly look around. I would be mortified if someone saw me crawling out my window. The window drops closed behind me with a snap. I say a little prayer that I can get back in as easily.

Trudging across the dewy grass toward the kitchen, I feel a bit self-conscious, walking around the property in the middle of the night. But it's peaceful. The moon lights my path and casts a delicate reflection in the lake.

I look a little farther across the pond and notice one of the other cabins has a light on. I stop for a moment, peering into the darkness. Shadows cross back and forth in front of the windows. I look at my watch. It's 2:00 a.m.

Why are people walking around at this hour?

A small breeze blows against my bare arms, and I shiver. A moment later, the light turns off, and the cabin is cast back into darkness.

I hope whoever was up didn't see me and think I was snooping around. I hurry to the kitchen bathroom, and thankfully it's unlocked. I do my business, close the door, and head back to my cabin.

To my relief, the window lifts open. I squeeze my body through the opening and fall back into the room. My heart is pounding from the experience, but after a few deep breaths, I fall back asleep.

My last thought is to ask Luis to fix the door.

6

"You okay?"

I fumble with the right words. Okay? Well, it's my third day here, and I'm standing staring at a colossal mess of burnt pans, clumps of dried and crusted sauces, and warped baking sheets.

What in the world happened here last night?

"Oh yeah, I'm fine," I say. I turn to see an older gray-haired man carrying a load of baking dishes. He drops them off by the sink.

"I'm Charlie." He extends his hand.

"Sadie," I say, wiping my hands before shaking his. "Nice to meet you."

"Likewise."

"Are you the pastry chef?"

"I am," he says. There's something about the crinkles in the corners of his eyes when he smiles that makes me instantly like him.

"What are you working on today?" I ask.

"Aw, well, we have a fresh crop of rhubarb coming in

from the garden today. So I'm making a strawberry and rhubarb tart topped with elderflower crème fraiche."

My mouth is literally watering.

"Maybe you can stop by my station for a tasting later?"

What I want to say is *heck yes!*

"Yes, that'd be great," I say with tempered enthusiasm.

Charlie smiles and walks back to his section of the kitchen. What I wouldn't give to have a position like Charlie's. The daily challenge of preparing fresh ingredients that call for innovative food design. Planning the dish, troubleshooting the presentation. I feel like a painter longing for a brush to complete her masterpiece. In a few minutes, the staff will meet in the dining room to go over the menu for the weekend, each chef presenting their ideas.

Maybe someday I'll be in that meeting. I plunge my hands into the mess before me as dirty dishwater sprays onto my apron. *But not today.*

Because of my previous work in a professional kitchen, I find the burnt pans to be a bit unusual. Typically, the staff work together as a team, and that includes rinsing off dishes and placing them in the sink area...without letting the charred food set in the pots and pans overnight.

It's as if someone made this mess for me on purpose.

Starting as a dishwasher wasn't exactly a part of my plan, but it's a start. Eventually I need to find a way to get my name in the roster of cooks. I'm guessing Luis will be my ticket in, since Norah barely looks at me, and Devon has barely been here. Luis seems to be the one who is truly running the restaurant.

I take a deep breath. Maybe Norah is working on some fantastic new dish, and this is part of her process. Judging by the pan in front of me, it was something made with a brown butter sauce. Who am I to question her genius?

Besides, after sleeping in a proper bed last night, I feel like a new woman. The knots in my shoulders and neck have dissolved. My brain feels more alert. I even managed to brew myself a decent cup of coffee this morning and bring it with me.

As I scour pans, I think about what I saw last night. Thankfully, I was able to get the front door open this morning, but I plan on bringing it up with Luis. But what about the cabin across the water? The whole situation was strange.

When he gave me a tour of the property on my first day, he didn't really mention who was staying in the cabins around the lake. Most of the staff have cars parked around the back, in the same lot where I park my own car. I observe them coming and going on a daily basis. Norah mentioned the cabins are under renovation, but aren't ready for guests. As far as I know, no one else is staying in one other than me.

Devon and Norah live in a beautifully restored carriage house behind the barn. The English-style landscaping with lavender bushes, wildflowers, and shrubs matches the front entrance of the property. It's equally charming. Perhaps Luis also lives on-site?

No sooner have I made a mental note to ask Luis about it, Devon suddenly appears at my elbow.

"Wow, what happened here?"

I shrug. "It was all here when I arrived. Maybe Norah's working on a new recipe?"

Devon snorts. "Maybe. Here, let me help you." He pulls an apron off a nearby wall hook and wraps it around his waist.

He grabs a few pans and starts scrubbing. I can feel the

heat from his skin and catch the faint smell of sandalwood. We stand side by side for a few minutes, working in unison, letting the sounds of the kitchen fill the silence between us.

"Devon!" Norah's cold voice cuts through the room. "What are you doing?"

He drops the pan he's working on and turns to face her. "I was just helping Sadie." He wipes his hands on the folds of his apron. "Is that a problem?"

"Well, no." Norah seems to bristle at his question. But by the scowl on her face, I'm guessing she doesn't approve. She's dressed in her signature top-to-bottom black attire, arriving in the room like a dark angel. "But I'm sure Sadie can handle the dishwashing by herself."

"Quite a mess she has here. Were you working in the kitchen last night?" Devon asks. For a moment, a bit of color rushes into Norah's cheeks. Her mouth twitches.

"I was with you, remember?" she says with a pointed stare. "Anyway, you're late for our kitchen meeting. I'll see you in the dining room."

Devon says nothing but responds with a nod. He turns and walks toward the door of the kitchen leading to the dining room. As I pull my gaze back to the sink, I notice a folded slip of paper on the floor. I bend down to pick it up.

I unfold it and see handwriting on the inside, instantly recognizing the structure of a recipe. Not wanting to draw attention to myself, I slip the paper into my pocket. I keep working for a few minutes and then take my bathroom break.

In the bathroom stall, I lock the door and reach into my apron. The list of ingredients is simple—sweet potatoes, chives, butter, and a few other items. On the flip side of the paper is a note that reads:

Norah's best. November 2018.

I chew the inside of my mouth. So this is a recipe from Pepper. From back when the place was at the peak of its success. I rub my fingers along the edge of the paper, which has a few food stains on it.

Why is Devon carrying this around?

A new idea bubbles up in my mind. What if I try to make this recipe? I have what I need equipment-wise in the cabin. I just need a few ingredients I can probably pull from leftovers in the kitchen.

I picture myself creating a masterpiece and presenting it to Devon. I know he's the key to getting my own restaurant, and maybe I could impress him by one-upping one of Norah's best recipes.

Or maybe not. I haven't even finished culinary school, after all.

I make a mental note to copy the recipe down and give it back to Devon. I'm sure Norah will be missing it soon.

The rest of the afternoon passes in a flurry of dishes and cleaning. The restaurant is full every night we're open, but after hearing the grumbles from the staff as they leave their meeting, I know we have an especially packed roster of guests. I plan to do my very best to help everyone.

About halfway through the shift, I hear Norah yelling from across the room.

"Where's the basil, Charlie? Are you completely incompetent? This dish is not complete without the basil. Didn't you see my notes?"

I look up to see Charlie and Norah at his station. His face is bright red. Everyone in the room seems to be quietly watching.

"I'm sorry, I must have run out," Charlie says.

Norah continues to scream at him. "Then we need to get some—now!"

She looks around the room, and when her eyes land on me, my heart practically stops.

"Sadie! Go out to the garden and get me some basil, now," she says, her eyes searing into me. "You do know what basil is, right?"

"Yes," I say. "Of course. I'll go now." I put down the glassware I was polishing and start walking toward the door.

"Everyone, back to work!" I hear Norah yell as I exit the kitchen. My heart beats wildly as I walk the dimly lit path toward the garden. I manage to pull some basil from the nearest section. I didn't have time to grab a pair of clippers, but this will have to do.

I hurry back to the kitchen. When I return, everyone is quietly working, and Norah is nowhere in sight. I drop a large pile of basil at Charlie's station.

"Are you okay?" I ask.

"I'm fine," he says, although his hands shake slightly as he takes the basil and runs it under some water in a nearby sink. "Just another day with Norah."

"Is she always like that?" I ask in a low whisper.

Charlie pauses and looks me in the eyes. "Always."

After that, he turns his back on me to start preparing the basil. I turn and walk back to my station, thankful I'm not yet under the kind of pressure Charlie is.

Or Norah, for that matter.

As I'm making my way through another stack of dishes, I feel my phone buzz in my pocket. And a few seconds later it buzzes again. With no family and few friends, I don't get a lot of messages.

Who would call me multiple times?

I take out my phone and swipe it open. The message makes my heart sink.

Brian Lagrange. My parole officer.

Why is it that when you finally start to make progress on your future, the past shows up to haunt you?

7

I decide to take a bathroom break and find some privacy so I can respond to the message. I don't want anyone looking over my shoulder. It's not like the message is a complete surprise, but I've been so caught up in my work here that I forgot to check in with Brian.

I'm on parole. A tiny little detail that I decided to omit from my résumé when I applied for the position here at Thistle. A piece of information that prevented me from getting almost every kitchen job I applied for over the last six months.

Except, of course, for Mike's Diner. And now here.

I stare at the messages.

Where you been, Sadie? We need to meet once a month, remember?

Sorry, I've been busy. New job.

Since when? You're supposed to check in with me. It's the law.

Ugh. I roll my eyes.

Sorry.

We'll talk about it tomorrow. Where would you like to meet?

My mouth goes dry. Well, there is no way he's coming here. I can't let the Winthrops find out about my prison time. That would ruin everything. There's only one place I can think of, and the thought of it makes my stomach twist in a knot.

Mike's?

I watch as the text bubble appears and disappears.

Sure. See you at 10am. Don't be late.

I text him back a thumbs-up. Mike's became the regular meeting place for Brian and me over the last few months. Mike himself didn't seem to care as long as I was off my regular shift. When I tried to offer Sally an explanation as to who Brian was and why we were meeting, she put her hand up to silence me. "Past is the past, kiddo. I don't need to know your business."

Sometimes I miss Sally, but I don't miss the diner. I'll take washing dishes at Thistle over the butt-slapping waitressing job any day. Not to mention the grease that clung to my hair for three days after I quit.

I leave the bathroom, make my way back to the mountain of pots and pans, and set to work again. As I pass the staff, I notice that everyone is quietly focused on their work.

There isn't a lot of chatter in this kitchen. It's not that the kitchen staff aren't friendly, it just feels like the stakes are higher here. One wrong move could set Norah off in the wrong mood. And I had a first-row seat to one of those mood swings today.

There are about a dozen cooks in total, plus myself, working in the kitchen on a daily basis. Dinners are served Thursday through Saturday while the rest of the week is dedicated to preparing the ingredients.

I have no doubt this place could be booked every night of the week. But now that I've been working here for a few weeks, I understand why they don't do it that way. Having an exclusive opening just a few nights a week allows for a truly unique experience for the guests. From the time their feet hit the gravel parking lot, which is part of the rural charm I suppose, they are catered to. And it gives the place a sort of reverence for its exclusivity. Not to mention the remote location requires some diners to travel for miles before they arrive.

Even though dinner service is only three nights, and because the staff here work all week to prepare, the dishes never stop coming in.

After a few minutes, the back door bursts open, and Devon re-enters the room. His face looks rather flushed. He walks over to one of the bakers and asks him if he saw a piece of paper lying on the floor. The man shakes his head no. Devon makes his way to the next station. Before he can say another word, I feel I should speak up.

"Devon?"

He looks at me and walks over. I don't really want to give the recipe back, but I've stared at it long enough to have the gist of the recipe memorized.

"Are you looking for this? You dropped it earlier."

His shoulders fall. "Yes! Thank you, Sadie, you saved me."

I can't help but bask in his praise. "You're welcome."

Ask him! I can hear some part of my brain screaming.

"I'd...well, I'd love to try to make it for you."

He cocks his head to the side, looking so intently into my eyes I almost take a step back. "Make the sweet potato soufflé?"

"I could try," I say, taking a step back. *Did I overstep?* "I went to CIA, and—"

He holds up a hand to silence me. "This is a complicated recipe. You must get the texture just right to make it work. But I appreciate your boldness."

He thinks I'm an idiot. "Oh, of course, I just thought—"

"I tell you what, we're actually closed this Thursday; how about you cook for me then? I know you're staying in cabin seven, and there's a full kitchen there. Seven o'clock sound good?"

"Yes, sir, that would be great. Thank you!"

Devon chuckles. "You don't need to call me sir. Devon is just fine."

He shoves the recipe back in his pocket, and as he turns he says, "See you then."

As soon as he leaves the room, I exhale deeply. My heart is pounding, and my palms are sweating. I am going to be cooking for one of the most famous restaurant investors in the Northeast. I can't believe it.

I return to my work with gusto, a stream of recipe ideas, twists, and ingredients running through my head.

8

"So tell me all about the new job. Pretty fancy place, right?" asks Brian.

"Yes," I say in response. I'm not going to waste an explanation about what a Michelin rating means to Brian, who thinks Mike's is the best food off the East-West Highway. "It's pretty fancy. One of the best in the country."

I'm sitting across from my parole officer in one of the booths near the front door of Mike's Diner the next morning. I'm down to monthly meetings with Brian, a stocky middle-aged man with tortoiseshell glasses. I was assigned to him right after I was released. From what I was told in prison, parole officers can be hit or miss. You either get someone who's a total jerk and wants to get you in trouble, or someone who actually wants to help.

Brian falls somewhere in the middle, depending on what kind of mood he's in. The sugar cream pie at Mike's usually helps sway him in the direction of helpful.

After I was released, he helped me find some subsidized housing and a waitressing job at Château Bernard. I didn't tell Brian about my exit from the restaurant, or why I left. He didn't ask either. I just told him to meet me at Mike's one day, and that was it.

I've also been lying to Brian about living out of my car.

Lying to a parole officer is a violation of parole. So is living out of your car. It wasn't easy to lie to Brian, but I also didn't want to have my parole status revoked either. The idea of going back to prison puts a sick feeling in my stomach.

Today, however, I'm feeling upbeat. I can with all honesty tell Brian about my new job and my new place. I can be honest and up front with him.

For the most part.

"I bet you don't miss this place," he says.

I shrug and take another sip of the piping hot coffee.

That's an understatement.

Just last week I was slinging biscuits and gravy to the customers. Now I'm working in the kitchen of one of the best restaurants in the country. As long as Norah doesn't fire me for looking at her the wrong way.

"I was lucky to get this job. But, yes, Thistle is great. The work there has been...satisfying."

"What exactly are you doing there?"

"Well, right now, I'm washing dishes." I'm not sure why I'm embarrassed to say this out loud. I'm sure Brian doesn't care what I'm doing at Thistle. "But there is room to move up to a cook position if I work hard."

"As long as you're working," he says between bites of his sugar cream pie. "So, where are you living?"

I chew my lip. Occasionally, parole officers will do a site visit to verify the residence of the parolee. In all my excitement, I hadn't thought about telling him where I'm staying. The last thing I need is Brian showing up at the cabin.

"I'm renting a cabin from the owner, Devon Winthrop."

Brian raises an eyebrow at me. He sits back deeper into the vinyl booth. "I'm going to need an address and a receipt for rent that verifies you live there."

My heart sinks. This is just what I was afraid of.

"Sure, I can get that for you." I tuck a strand of hair behind my ear. "But I'm new there, so it may take me a few days."

He cocks his head to the side, as if trying to read me. As a parole officer, I'm sure Brian is pretty good at reading people. And I'm sure he can tell when they're lying. He stares at me for what feels like an eternity as I squirm in my seat.

"Okay, I'm going to hold you to that," he finally says.

"Great," I say, letting out a small breath. At least I've bought myself some time. "I'm actually cooking for Devon tonight," I blurt out.

A funny look crosses his face. "Just the two of you?"

"I think so."

"Hmm. Be careful around men like that, Sadie."

I sit up in my seat. "What do you mean?"

"Listen, I wasn't going to say anything, but I had a client who worked at Pepper." He puts his fork down next to his plate and pushes it away. "And I looked into the Winthrops as well. There are rumors."

My stomach twists in a knot. "Rumors about what?"

"It would be unprofessional of me to discuss another client," he says, leaning forward. "But do you know why Pepper closed?"

"It was a fire, right?"

"Yes. A fire that destroyed the restaurant and half the building. Supposedly no one was injured. But the Winthrops lost everything. The staff went unpaid. The building was condemned. And they never reopened."

I listen intently. I knew there was a fire, and then the Winthrops sort of disappeared from the culinary world for a while. But I never really thought much of it. Thistle opened up with a splash of news, and the fire was kind of forgotten.

"Maybe they just took the insurance money and needed a break. Restaurants are hard work."

"Or maybe there was no insurance money."

I purse my lips together. *Where is he going with this?*

"I'm sure it was insured. Otherwise, how were they able to open Thistle?"

Brian sits back in his seat and shrugs. "That's all I'm going to say. I'm just warning you to tread carefully. Don't get too close to the Winthrops." He presses a napkin to his lips. "You have more to lose than they do."

My stomach knots up at his words. Of course, I would do anything to avoid going back to prison. But I can't see how working for the Winthrops could get me in any kind of trouble. I'm working at one of the most famous restaurants in the country, and they've given me a place to sleep on top of it. It's more than I ever hoped for when I got out of the pen.

"Hey, Brian. You two finished up here?"

Sally walks up to our table. She looks more tired than usual, her hair slightly oily from lack of washing. One of the other servers mentioned she's been covering my shifts since Mike's niece took over the kitchen. Apparently Rebecca can only cook now that she has a baby in tow.

"Yup, I need to head out. You serve the best pie here, Sally."

"Well, thanks, sugar."

I stack our plates together for Sally to take them away.

"Stop by and say hi on your way out, Sadie. I need to talk to you."

"Okay, sure," I reply.

Brian is already on his feet. "I'll need your address and a receipt for rent next week. Or else we'll need to set up a site visit so I can verify residence."

"I'll get it to you as soon as possible," I say, rising to my feet. "I promise."

Brian gives me a look that makes me feel like he can see right through to my soul. "I'm sure you will. Bye, Sadie."

"Bye," I manage. My guts feel like spaghetti. I mean, technically I have nothing to hide from him. It's just the fact that the Winthrops still don't know about my prison time. And I need to keep that a secret for as long as possible.

I watch him walk out, the bell clanging against the metal door as he steps into the sunshine. *What is he not telling me about Thistle?*

I hadn't given much thought to the three-year gap between the closing of Pepper and the opening of Thistle. And why wouldn't the Winthrops have insurance? It's really none of my business. But part of me is curious. What if Devon offers me a more permanent position at Thistle? I thought the Winthrops had loads of money.

I look back toward the kitchen and see Sally bounding out the swinging door, her arms full of dishes. I could see if she wants some help, but in truth I am exhausted. I want to have enough time to stop by the farmer's stand on Highway 24 so I can pick up some ingredients to cook for Devon. Not to mention I need to be back at work.

"Sadie!" I hear a voice belt my name from across the room. I turn on my heel to see Joe, the semitruck driver who humiliated me a few weeks ago. He's waving at me from one of the corner booths. I pretend not to see him.

It's definitely time to get out of here.

I catch Sally's attention and mouth the words *I have to go. See you soon.*

Call me, she calls back as she lays down four full plates in front of her customers.

I push my way out the door and walk to my car. Questions from my conversation with Brian float through my head. No insurance money? How did they cover their losses from the fire? I take a deep breath and shake my head.

It's really none of my business.

Besides, I only have one question I need an answer for right now—how am I going to top Norah's best soufflé?

9

"Come on in," I say, opening the door.

Devon Winthrop crosses the threshold into the cabin. I'm still pinching myself. I'm also sweating through my shirt. Our dinner is purely professional, but I find myself biting my lip as the fresh hint of sandalwood floats off his skin and into the room. I tried to clean myself up after feverishly working for the last two hours on the sweet potato soufflé I found in Norah's recipe. It was a little tricky, but I managed.

I pulled my hair back at the sides and put on a clean sweater and slacks a few minutes before he arrived. I even put on some perfume to mask the sweat.

"It smells amazing in here," Devon says as he walks into the kitchen. There's a small table in the room with four chairs. I lit a few candles to give it the ambience the meal hopefully deserves, but the effect feels a little too intimate. Beads of sweat pop up on my nose.

"Thank you," I say. I tuck a strand of curly hair behind my ears and rearrange the candles I set on the table. Devon pulls out a chair and seats himself. He's brought a bottle of wine.

"I hope you don't mind; it's been a long day," he says, nodding his head at the bottle.

"No, it's fine," I say, grabbing the bottle from the table. "Here, let me open that for you."

I turn my back to him as I take a few steps to the kitchen. He sits in silence as I fumble through the drawers, looking for a bottle opener. Bottle in hand, I turn around to face him while I pry it open. He's on his phone, a frown on his face.

"Is Norah going to join us?" I ask timidly.

"Hmm?" he says, obviously immersed in some important business on his phone. He looks up at me and gives me a tight smile. "Oh, Norah is with Luis, chasing down some mussels from a supplier. They had to drive to the coast, so she'll be back tomorrow."

I pull a glass from the cabinet and set it in front of Devon. He looks up from his phone.

"Please pour yourself a glass," he says, eyes on the bottle in front of him. He gives me a crooked smile. "It might help calm your nerves."

I feel a bit of heat rush to my cheeks. Since this is my first time cooking for Devon, I wasn't quite sure what the protocol would be. Are we eating together? Do I simply serve him?

I turn away to pull another glass from the cabinet. The bottle he brought is a 2018 Caymus Cabernet. From what I remember from working at Château Bernard, it costs a few hundred dollars a bottle. I know just enough about wine to create pairings, but I don't drink too much of it myself. I guess I'll make an exception for tonight.

"Norah seems really dedicated to her work. I admire that," I say, filling up the glasses halfway.

A curious look crosses his face. He almost snorts as he brings the glass to his lips. "You could say that," he says.

I place my glass on the table and turn back to the kitchen. I spent some time creating a small appetizer to start the meal. When I offered to cook Devon the soufflé, I knew I would need to do more than just one recipe to impress him.

"Here's a little amuse-bouche to open up your palate." I set a white ceramic spoon in front of him. "It's pickled watermelon with cilantro and a bit of goat cheese."

Devon leans forward and lifts the spoon into his mouth.

"Hmm, delicious," he says as he places the spoon back on the table.

I turn and head back to the kitchen to prepare the next course. Devon stands and follows me.

"Can I help?"

I'm already so nervous I feel like I could throw up. I was hoping he would bring Norah so they could chat while I finish cooking. Not that Norah would make me feel any more comfortable, but having Devon's full attention on me is about as much pressure as I can take.

"No, I'm fine, thanks. Everything is almost ready."

"Right," he says, returning to his seat. "I think there's a Bluetooth speaker around here somewhere. Let me see if I can put on some music."

I put some finishing touches on the creme sauce while Devon connects the speaker. A few moments later, some light jazz is floating through the air. I probably would have picked something a little more modern, but the sounds are calming.

I pull the soufflé from the oven, along with a flood of

steam that hits me in the face. To my relief, the soufflé has a fluffy crown, and I gently place the tray with water on the counter. I use a sifter to dust the top with a special blend of spices I created to bring the flavor of the sweet potato to life. As I plate the dish, Devon walks back over to the kitchen.

"Plating for one? Why don't you join me?"

I did create two soufflés just in case one didn't make it. "Okay, if you don't mind."

"I insist," he says. He touches the small of my back, his breath tickling my neck. I nearly shiver. "Here, let me help you."

He reaches over to grab one of the plates from the counter and carries it to the table. I carefully pour the pan sauce I made into a small ramekin and follow him. As is customary at a Michelin-style restaurant, I present my dish.

"This is a sweet potato soufflé with caramelized leeks, rhubarb, and dusted with pulverized cane sugar and cinnamon."

"Thank you, chef," Devon says, smiling up at me from his seat. I feel a little flutter in my stomach. I'm not sure if it's because this is the first time someone has called me chef, or if it's the charming smile on his face.

I hear a small voice in my head. *Focus, Sadie. He's married!*

I sit down quietly across from him, holding my breath as he lifts the fork to his mouth. I can't even bring myself to take a bite of my dish. Seconds feel like hours as I watch his face for any expression of satisfaction...or disappointment.

"Hmm, this is really great, Sadie. I can taste a hint of the leeks, and the spices are not too overpowering. And the texture is..." He leans back in his chair. I hold my breath. "Perfect."

I feel my whole body melt back into my chair. "Thank you," I say as I exhale.

Devon reaches for his wine. "So, tell me why you quit CIA?"

"I couldn't afford tuition. So I took some time off. I thought I could get some real-world experience and come back and finish later."

"And did you?"

I pick up my wineglass and hesitate before taking a sip, tapping my fingers against the glass. I know I won't be driving anywhere, and besides, one glass of wine is perfectly safe, but I don't drink much anymore. Not since that night. But Devon smiles at me, so I grip the glass more firmly and take a sip.

"Yes, I worked at Château Bernard. And now here. I'm hoping to save up enough money to head back to school next fall."

Devon cocks his head to the side. "With a soufflé like this, you may not even need to finish school. This is outstanding."

I feel myself beaming under his praise. I'm also starting to relax a bit, probably the wine hitting my nearly empty stomach.

"What you've done here with Thistle—it's amazing. You and Norah must be very proud."

Devon looks away as he speaks. "It's been a journey. But it feels like things are really starting to come together. After what happened at Pepper, I wasn't sure if we'd ever own a restaurant again."

"Really? I mean, Pepper was incredible. It was on every best restaurant list in the country." I take a small bite of my soufflé, which melts in my mouth. I can't help but feel a little pinch of pride. "It's not like the fire was anyone's fault."

When he turns his face back toward me, his expression looks troubled. Just as I'm about to backtrack and apologize for bringing it up, Devon's phone buzzes on the table. He looks down and furrows his brow.

"Excuse me, I need to take this."

"Of course," I say. Devon stands up from the table and walks to the door. I clean up the plates from the table, leaving the wine. I can hear Devon outside talking in a low tone as he paces in front of the window. The sun has mostly set, and it's well past dusk. Time sort of froze while he was here, and I realize that it's probably getting late.

As I'm placing the dishes in the sink to soak, I hear Devon's voice grow louder. I step a little closer to the door to listen, without listening of course.

"No! I mean, no, you don't need to come here." There's a pause. "I'll get you the money, but you don't need to come. The staff can't see anyone or know anything, not if you ever want the money."

I move my fingers toward my mouth, intending to bite my nails. I stop. Whom does he owe money to? Why doesn't he want them to come here?

It's really none of my business. I just have to put up with this for two years. I just need to survive and gain experience until my background check clears. Then I can move on without having to lie on my résumé.

The conversation I had with Brian earlier today about the Winthrops is niggling in my mind. If Brian was right about the insurance, how were the Winthrops able to afford this place? I know they have loads of money, mostly from

Devon's family, but it must have cost a fortune to get this place up and running. Especially if they had to eat the cost of the fire at Pepper.

I refocus my attention on dessert. I made a fresh lemon mint and herb sorbet last night with a blender I borrowed from the restaurant kitchen, and carefully molded it into a small cylinder using a spring pan I borrowed from the main kitchen. But I'm not sure how long Devon's conversation will take, so I'm hesitant to pull it from the freezer.

I stand there, unsure what to do. The dinner seems to be going well, but I can feel my anxiety rising with each passing minute Devon is still pacing outside my door. Just as I'm about to sit down and have another sip of wine, he walks back into the room.

His expression is harder than when he left.

"Everything okay?" I ask gingerly.

He combs his hand through his hair. "Fine," he says as he walks toward the small table. "I may need another glass of wine."

I watch as he sits down and pours himself a full glass. It's definitely more than the five-ounce pour we were instructed to give to our guests at Château Bernard. I hesitate for a moment.

"I made a lemon herb sorbet for dessert. Would you like to try some?"

Devon picks up his glass of wine and practically guzzles it down. Any sommelier worth their salt would be horrified at the sight of him not savoring every sip. I finger the sleeve of my sweater as I watch him, waiting for a response.

"Maybe just a bite," he says as he places the glass on the table. His cheeks are slightly flushed, probably a sign that the wine has gone to his head. When I serve his dessert, he immediately picks up his spoon and takes a bite.

"Amazing, Sadie," he says. "Truly."

"Would you like some coffee or espresso?"

"Another time." He waves his hand. "Thank you for having me tonight. It was..." He tips his head slightly, and a small smile reaches his lips. "Delicious. You've helped me see what's possible."

Is he drunk?

"I was happy to do it. Maybe I'll get a chance to work with Luis sometime."

"It's very possible," he says, his eyes boring into mine. Then he stands up from the table. "I've got a bit of business to take care of in my office."

He walks to the door. I follow him and hold the door open as he prepares to leave. He turns and looks me in the eyes, then chuckles.

"You have a little bit of sauce on your cheek." He reaches over and runs his thumb along my jaw. I feel my heartbeat lighten.

"Oh," I say, touching my cheek after he drops his hand. "Happens all the time." I let out a nervous laugh.

We make eye contact. The way he's looking at me, it's almost as if he's...I'm not sure what he's going to do. For a moment, my mind flashes to Peter. And what it took to get here. I take a step back.

"Well, good night, Sadie," he says, mirroring my movement.

"Good night," I say, taking another step away from the door. He gives me one more half smile before ducking out the door.

I close the door and let all the air out of my lungs,

leaning with my back against the door. The food wasn't perfect, but it wasn't a total disaster. Devon seemed to be genuinely impressed.

The only problem? I think I might have a crush on my boss.

And the worst part is, I think he feels the same way.

10

When I enter the kitchen the next morning, I'm practically walking on a cloud. After Devon left, I put on some of the same jazz music and cleaned the tiny cabin kitchen until it was spotless. I was so filled with adrenaline from the success of the evening I could hardly sit down.

It wasn't until midnight that I finally fell asleep. I woke up this morning feeling refreshed and ready to take on anything Norah might throw my way.

"We need the mushrooms, now!" Norah screams from across the room, right on cue.

It's Friday evening now, and we're serving the last group of reservations for the evening. Norah has been unusually tense, screaming and yelling at nearly every member of staff. Barely a word has been spoken throughout the night except for hushed conversations between the line cooks to make sure everything goes out on time.

Tonight's menu includes a sausage and mushroom croquette served with lamb and pickled radishes, and also

Cornish lobster with heirloom tomatoes and avocado. The steam from the lobster, coupled with the butter sauce warming in the pot, makes my mouth water.

The biggest challenge I face this evening is that Norah requires both be served on a six-inch square plate. And for some reason, we only have a dozen of these available.

Which means I'm running back and forth behind the service line and around the kitchen, trying to grab enough of these to keep them clean and ready to be plated. The effort has been exhausting, and my feet are already swollen and sore.

I'm getting ready to rush another round of plates over to the meat prep station when Norah turns around and slams into me. The half a dozen plates I'm holding crash to the ground and shatter on the floor. I catch my breath. Norah's face turns red.

"Sadie! What the hell are you doing?"

"I'm so sorry, Norah. I'll clean this up right away," I say as I hunker down to the ground and start picking up plate shards.

"I know we plucked you from the truck stop down the road, but you've got to do better! Did you think you can just stumble around like an idiot? Watch where you're going next time!" She gestures to the broken plates on the floor. "I want this mess cleaned up now!"

My cheeks burn as I lean down and continue to pick up the shards. Norah moves to the other side of the workstation and helps prep the Cornish lobsters. A cook named Alex comes over with a broom to help me sweep up the smaller pieces.

As I reach for one of the shards, I slice my finger. I feel a bit dizzy as I see my own blood squirt onto the floor. I pull out a rag that I had tucked into my apron and quickly wipe up the blood, then pull a clean towel off a nearby counter to wrap up my finger. I'm afraid Norah might see the blood and yell at me for bleeding on her floor.

Needless to say, Norah is not the mentor I was hoping for when I dreamed of working at Thistle. And now she has announced to all the staff that I was working at a truck stop. Just when I was starting to gain the respect of the staff for working my butt off, now they just think I'm some lowly dishwasher.

I manage to get the mess of broken plates cleaned up in just a few minutes, although I'm sure there are a few small pieces hiding under the worktables. I need to run to the bathroom and clean the cut on my finger.

"Sadie! I need six of the six-inch square plates, right now. We are ready to plate! Where are they?"

I pop my head up from the floor. "I'm sorry, they're broken."

The look Norah gives me sends a cold shiver down my spine. For a moment, I think she might take the knife she's holding and fling it at me. Her eyes widen.

"Then go to the storage room and get more plates." She points at the side door of the kitchen with her knife. "Do you think you can manage that, or do I need to hold your hand?"

"Yes, I can manage," I say meekly. I jump to my feet and walk as quickly as I can toward the door. I hold my hand down at my side so she can't see the rag wrapped around my finger. As I walk out of the room, I can hear Norah telling the meat station cook to keep the lobster in the warming drawer until I return. I pick up my speed.

I make it to the storage room in half the time it normally takes me. The room is a large L shape, and the dishware storage is in the back corner. With one hand, I open the flaps of the boxes at the back one at a time to find the right plates. After looking through about five boxes, I find what I need.

Why did no one tell me there was an entire box of these in storage? I roll my eyes and groan. That would have made my night so much easier. It's difficult with one hand, but I manage to balance a small box of the plates on my right forearm.

Just as I turn to head back to the kitchen, I hear two people enter the room.

"I can't keep doing this, Devon." That's Luis's voice. The door clicks shut. I freeze for a few seconds, the box of plates still teetering on my arm. I take a step back around the corner where they won't see me.

"I told you before, it's only temporary. Once we pay off the debt—" I can hear Devon's voice, but I can't see his face. I take another step deeper into the corner of the room.

"Pay off the debt? How can we pay off the debt when we keep spending more money? We added the greenhouse, and now the cabin renovations. When does it stop?"

"Listen, Luis, you let me worry about how to run the business. All you have to do is keep the kitchen running smoothly. I've got enough cash saved up so we can pay off our debt in just a couple of months. As long as the customers stay happy, we're good."

"Do you really think it's a good idea to keep that much cash on the property?"

"It's safe, trust me."

I hear Luis let out a huffed breath. "But we're lying to everyone," he says in a low voice. "I hate lying. It feels wrong."

"Is that right? You didn't seem to have a problem lying about your green card, did you?"

"You were supposed to help me with that."

"I did my best. Immigration laws are tricky. Remember that."

"You're a—"

A sharp knock at the door cuts Luis off. My heart beats a little faster.

"Yes?" Devon says.

"We have a problem with one of the customers at table twelve; can you help?" I hear one of the members of staff ask.

"I'll be right there," Devon says. I hear the door click shut again. "Don't mess this up, Luis. I don't think either of us will enjoy the food they serve in prison."

Prison?

I nearly drop the box of plates. My hand is throbbing at this point, but I'm afraid to move. There's a beat of silence as I hear footsteps exit the room and the door close. I let out a long breath and make my way around the corner. To my relief, they're both gone. I hurry down the hall and back into the kitchen.

Norah is nowhere to be seen. Another exhale.

I drop off the plates at the prep station and scurry back to the dishwashing station. There's a first aid kit next to the sink. I pull out a few bandages and wrap my finger, then place a plastic glove over it and wince as it pulls on the cut.

After a few minutes, the adrenaline has worked its way out of my system. I feel exhausted and stare out the window as my hands move mechanically over the dishes.

The sun is just a few seconds from dropping below the horizon. The cabin in the far distance is illuminated against the failing light. Inside, there's a small lamp glowing through the window.

After drying my hands, I absently finger my collarbone, watching the sun set. The Winthrops are hiding something. Something big. It turns out I'm not the only one keeping secrets.

11

Today, I'm determined to impress Norah, whatever it takes. I've filled up on espresso and pulled my hair back in a tight bun. So it's a bit shocking when I walk up to my cleaning station to find someone else cleaning the dishes. A young man wearing a white apron, jeans, and Adidas sneakers. The bounce in my step goes flat, and I take a few slow steps toward him, then tap on his shoulder.

"Um, excuse me, I'm Sadie. This is my workstation," I say with a forced smile. He tips his head to the side as if trying to understand what I'm saying.

"Sorry, no English."

I bite my lip. *Great.*

"Luis?" I say, hoping he knows where he is.

"Sí, por alla," he replies, nodding to the far corner of the kitchen. I turn in that direction, and to my relief, Luis is speaking with one of the cooks. I make a beeline for him, my heart pounding in my chest.

It's obvious I have been replaced. *But have I been fired?*

I tap him on the shoulder. "Luis, can you help me? There's someone at my station."

Luis turns around and looks at me with a warm expression. He has a warm glow on his cheeks. There's something different about him, but I can't quite put my finger on it.

"Oh, Sadie, I'm so glad you're here," he says, touching my arm. "Listen, you've sort of been promoted."

This is it, I think. *I'm finally going to cook in the Thistle kitchen.*

"Devon thought it would be good for you to learn more about our menu, and two of our servers have called in sick. So you'll be waiting on our guests this evening."

My cheeks flush with heat. *What?! I'm going to wait tables?*

"Waiting tables?"

The last job I want is to serve food to the guests. I didn't go to culinary school so I could bounce around from one waitressing job to another. Not to mention, waiting tables makes me feel self-conscious. Not that the guests at Thistle will be anything like the slobs at Mike's Diner. I doubt anyone will be smacking me on the butt on the way back to the kitchen. But still, I'd prefer to be creating food, not serving it.

"Listen," Luis says, lowering his voice. "This is a good thing. You'll get to know the menu like the back of your hand. And you can get direct feedback from our guests on what they like and don't like."

"Okay," I say, still uncertain as to why I'm going to be serving tables. Did I not just wow Devon with my cooking skills? I thought I was on my way to line cook.

Now I'm going to wait tables?

"Ingrid is our front-of-house manager. She'll get you up to speed. The staff are meeting in fifteen minutes. There are uniforms in the hall closet. You can go and find one in your size before the pre-shift meeting."

He turns his attention back to the cook, signaling the end of the conversation. My eyes sting with disappointment, but I swallow my pride and head to the uniform closet.

I keep my head down as I walk down the hallway. All the excitement from the success of the other night has been swept down the drain. I try to tell myself to be patient, but working at the front of the restaurant rather than back in the kitchen feels like a huge step back.

What is Devon thinking?

Just as I'm about to open the door to pick out one of the fitted denim uniforms, a voice stops me in my tracks.

"Sadie!"

I turn around to see Norah looking me up and down with her glaring green eyes.

"Hi, Norah," I say, forcing a smile.

"I'm glad I caught you. I think it's wonderful you'll be working as a server with us for a while. It will really give you a chance to get to know our menu," she says with a forced cheerful voice. I think her goal is to sound positive, but it just comes across as fake.

"Right," I say, not even trying to hide my disappointment. "It's just, I thought maybe I was going to cook..."

"Cook? Like you cooked for my husband?" Norah raises her eyebrows at me. I feel my cheeks burn for the second time today.

"Well—"

"I think serving our guests is the best place for you right now. Besides, with your *serving experience*, I'm sure you'll do great," she says.

Serving experience.

What did she mean by that? She knows I was working at Mike's when she hired me. Maybe it was just another dig at my crappy diner job. Or maybe she found out the truth. That I wasn't working in the Château Bernard kitchen, I was actually waiting tables.

And sleeping with my boss, Peter. The restaurant world can be painfully small. And people love to gossip.

"Now," she says, her smile sickly sweet, "is there something we can do about your appearance? Maybe a little blush and mascara? We want you to look your best for our guests, right?"

"Right," I say, touching the bun on my head. "Of course."

"Good." She pats me on the arm as she walks past, back toward the kitchen.

Norah seems to have a way of humiliating me every time I turn around. And why is she so worried about my appearance? I quickly go through the uniform closet to find a uniform. I'm going to have to run back to the cabin to put on some makeup before the pre-shift meeting.

As I enter the storage room, I see four or five other waiters thumbing through the rows of plastic-wrapped uniforms hanging neatly against the wall. I awkwardly search for a size medium, side by side with the rest of the staff.

I pull out my size, rip off the plastic wrapping and toss it in the trash on my way out the door. As I run back to the cabin, Norah's words tumble through my mind like clothes in a washing machine.

I rip open the door to the cabin and make my way to the bathroom, where I've stashed my cosmetic bag.

As I brush on mascara and dust some blush on my cheeks, I try to talk myself off the ledge of paranoia I'm about to leap from. Surely I'm overthinking this. I mean, she knows I worked at the diner, and that's serving experience.

And if she knows I slept with Peter, so what? It's not like he was married or anything. But he does know something about me Norah doesn't. He knows I went to prison.

And if Norah finds out about that, I'm seriously screwed.

12

"And remember, any questions about wine, you must always defer to our sommelier," says Ingrid, our restaurant manager. She's been prattling on about service for more than forty-five minutes. I'm doing my best to stay focused, but my stomach is grumbling, and my mind keeps wandering back to the kitchen.

We're sitting around one of the largest tables in the restaurant, about a half dozen of us, having our pre-shift meeting. I've been through the Thistle dining room a few times before, but never in the evening when the sun is beginning to set. Candles are lit around me, casting a soft glow on the worn wood floors. Fresh wildflowers mixed with artichokes, carrots, and—*of course*—thistles are artfully set in the center of each table. The white linens are expertly pressed, and the silver freshly polished.

My heartbeat has finally slowed down after sprinting across the farm to make it here on time. I reach up to rub my eye, then realize I'm wearing mascara. It's strange. I've barely worn makeup since I've been here, since the steam from the dishwasher pretty much melts it off my face.

The only consolation I have for serving versus washing dishes in the back is that I'll probably make more from a night's worth of tips here than an entire week working back in the kitchen. The tips are split evenly between all the servers, and I'm sure everyone is sizing me up and hoping I don't blow it for the rest of them.

As Ingrid prattles on about "a step above the highest level of service you've ever had," I can't help but wonder what Norah meant by her comment. Does she know about the deal I made with Peter? What else does she know about me?

If she knew I went to prison, I'd already be fired, right?

"And finally, I wanted to welcome Sadie to our crew this evening. Sadie has been working with us in the kitchen and is filling in for Adam and Darcie, who are both sick. I want you all to help her get up to speed and be available to answer any questions."

I look around the table and smile, with a meek wave. The waitstaff seems less than enthusiastic about my presence. They pretty much glare at me from around the table.

"All right then, everyone off to do their pre-shift work. Our first reservation arrives in thirty minutes."

Before she's even finished, everyone is on their feet and bustling off to different corners of the restaurant. I watch two female servers whisper to each other as they leave. I can only catch a few words, but it's enough to make me cringe.

"I heard she's staying in one of the cabins." She lowers her voice to a whisper. "And Devon has been visiting her at night."

Oh no.

Before I can give their comments another thought, Ingrid is clearing her throat. It's just her and me left at the table. Her rigid posture and slicked-back hair remind me of a school mistress. All she's missing is a ruler. Not to mention her narrow blue eyes, which always seem to be scowling at me.

Those eyes are boring into me now.

"Do you think you can handle this tonight, Sadie? Any questions?"

I pull my shoulders back. "Yes, I think I can handle it. I've waited tables before."

Hopefully my experience at Château Bernard is enough to get me through the evening.

She gives me a stiff nod. "I'm assuming you have studied the menu? You know every detail and are prepared for every question?"

"Yes," I say. That I can say with confidence. I've pretty much obsessed over the menu.

"Good. Remember, you must constantly be in movement. Sweeping crumbs, refilling glasses, and anticipating every need of the customer." She brushes back a tiny hair over her ear. "There is no room for error."

She narrows her eyes at me. My mouth goes dry. I definitely don't want to be on the wrong side of this woman's approval.

"I will do my best. Thanks for this opportunity," I say. She straightens her sleeve and clucks her tongue.

"Well, we didn't have much of a choice. But Norah thinks you can handle yourself." She stands up from the table. "I hope she's right."

With that, she turns and leaves the room. *And I thought Norah was cold.*

I stand up from the table and head to the hostess stand to receive my table assignments. To my relief, I only have two tables for the evening, both near the kitchen. This should be a breeze.

"SADIE, NOW!" I hear one of the servers barking at me from the kitchen. As it turns out, being a server at Thistle is a little more complex than I anticipated. Even though I spent a couple of years working at Château Bernard, let's face it, I am a little rusty.

Mike's Diner didn't do me any favors.

The tables I'm serving range from groups of two to four. One couple in particular has me running all over the restaurant for random requests, like showing them some of the dessert plates that we use here, and getting a certain size cube of ice for his old-fashioned. Another set of couples has had a little too much wine. The women are laughing loudly, and one of the men is definitely flirting with me.

The starched denim shirt I donned at the beginning of the shift is now wrinkled and clinging to my damp skin. Every few minutes Ingrid stops in to check on my progress. She keeps a stoic expression, and I can't tell if she's pleased with me or disappointed. I guess I'll find out by the end of the evening.

It's nearly nine o'clock when the restaurant finally starts winding down. Out of about forty tables in the dimly lit room, only four remain occupied. My last table is finishing their dessert of sorbet with pickled peaches and flaxseed crisp. I stop by their table once more before I'm finally able to make a break for the restroom.

I keep my gaze forward as I pass through the dining room toward the bathroom in the hallway. Just as I'm about to push open the door and leave the dining room, I catch the sound of a name I haven't heard in a very long time.

Samantha.

For a moment I hesitate, my hand suspended in front of the swinging door. I hear the name again, then rush through the door, hoping that whoever it is, they haven't seen my face. My heartbeat speeds up as I walk toward the bathroom. I bust through a stall door and close it securely behind me.

Did I really just hear that? *Am I imagining things?*

I hurry through my business, but as I'm washing my hands, I freeze at the sight of my own reflection.

Samantha.

I could have sworn someone called me by that name. Then I realize I've been standing in front of the mirror with water just running over my hands for who knows how long. The door to the bathroom swings open. I recognize one of the servers. She's taller than me, with long legs and a perfectly sculpted bun that sits at the base of her skull. I think her name is Jessica, but I'm not one hundred percent sure. Her eyes go slightly wide when she sees me.

"Are you okay?" she says. "You look like you've seen a ghost."

If you only knew.

"I'm feeling a little sick," I say as I turn off the water.

"Oh," she says, staring at me. There are a few seconds of awkward silence.

"I'm Sadie."

"Right, I remember. I'm Jessica."

I get the distinct feeling that Jessica does not like me. But I have no other options at this point.

"Listen, I know I'm new, but is there any chance you could pick up the check at table nineteen? They're finished, but I'm afraid..." I touch my stomach to emphasize my predicament.

She narrows her eyes and studies me for a moment.

"Sure," she says, tipping her chin at me. "But you owe me. No one gets a free ride around here just because the boss likes us." She looks me up and down. "Some of us worked years to get a job like this."

Wow, that was harsh. I straighten up. "Of course, I promise I'll pay you back," I say.

"Let me just use the restroom first," she says as she passes me to enter the stall. I splash some water on my cheeks. Now I see why everyone at the pre-shift meeting was staring at me. They think I just walked into this job because I'm the boss's favorite. But which boss? Norah's made it clear she's not too fond of me, even though she hired me.

They must all think I'm sleeping with Devon.

Which isn't true, of course. Not that I haven't thought about it. He's quite handsome. And the way he looks at me sometimes...

No, no, I push those thoughts to the back of my mind. I've got bigger problems to worry about.

Jessica comes out, washes her hands, and heads out the door. As she leaves, she says over her shoulder, "Hope you feel better."

Her words couldn't be less sincere. I don't miss much about Mike's Diner, but I could use a little bit of Sally right now.

I take a few minutes to collect myself before heading back to the kitchen to do my post-shift work. I try to dismiss the Samantha incident from earlier. Surely I'm imagining things. There's absolutely no one from my past who would ever have the chance to eat at a place like Thistle. I think the pressure I've put myself under is starting to take a toll on my brain.

I finish the server tasks for the evening on autopilot. Ingrid tells me that I've done well and gives me a few pointers for my next shift. I consider this a win, since I doubt Ingrid gives out many compliments. So I still have a job, which is good.

I'm beyond exhausted when I finally arrive back at the cabin. My phone is plugged into the wall on the nightstand. I tap the screen half-heartedly before falling into bed.

I see a few missed calls from Sally. *Why would Sally be calling me?*

I know I should call her back right away, but I decide to close my eyes for just a few minutes first. Before I know it, I'm fast asleep with the phone lying on my chest.

13

I sit straight up in my bed and clasp my chest. A sound from outside broke me out of a light sleep. I look around and realize it's still dark outside. My phone blinks at me, stating it's 2:00 a.m. I take two deep breaths in and let them out slowly.

Why am I so cold? I look down and realize I fell asleep on top of the sheets. It's slightly chilly in the cabin, which would explain why I couldn't go into a deep slumber.

I stand up to pull the sheets and bedcover back. As I do, a small light catches my eye outside the window. That must be the source of the sound that woke me. I had the wherewithal to draw the curtains closed before I fell asleep, but they never quite shut all the way. I take a few steps toward the window and peer into the darkness.

It's not completely dark. The moon is sparkling like a shiny nickel in the night sky, gently reflected on the small lake on the property. The lone cabin in the distance, the one that had the light on the first night I stayed here—has its lights on again.

I still haven't had a chance to ask Devon who's staying there. Every time we're together, it sort of slips my mind. But I'm drawn to it regardless. I take a step closer to peer through the window. As my eyes adjust to the darkness, I can make out two dark figures near the barn on the far side of the lake. I assume it's Norah and Devon, maybe out for a walk.

But in the middle of the night?

I catch the faint sounds of their raised voices, but it's too far for me to hear clearly with the window closed. I squint my eyes. Norah seems to point toward the cabin in the back with the light on. Devon throws his hands up in the air. He takes a step forward, and she takes a step back. Moonlight hits his face, and I realize it's not Devon in the dark with Norah—it's Luis.

What are the two of them fighting about at two a.m.? I watch for a few more seconds, wrestling with the idea of shutting the curtain and going back to bed. I know I shouldn't be snooping on them. But I can't stop watching. Just as I'm about to grab the curtains and pull them totally closed, I see Luis touch Norah's face.

And suddenly the two of them are kissing.

I feel my mouth drop open. *What is going on?*

The two figures have now merged into one as they make out in the moonlight. I rub my eyes, thinking maybe I'm still in some sort of dream state. But no, it's definitely real.

Luis and Norah are having an affair.

I take a self-conscious step back into the cabin, away from the window. I don't want to be involved in this. And I definitely don't want to know what's going on between them. I take one last look out the window and see the two of them making their way into the barn. If their body language is any indication, I know what's going to happen next.

I lie back down on the bed, this time under the sheets. *Norah and Luis.* I didn't see that coming. Does Devon know? I feel bad for him, thinking back to when he went to kiss her in the kitchen, but she turned away. Now I know why.

As I will myself back to sleep, a few new ideas float around in my head. But this time I'm not thinking about soufflés or how I might use the batch of fresh truffles we're receiving on Thursday for a new recipe.

I'm thinking of how I might use this secret to my advantage.

14

A sharp knock on the door wakes me the next morning. I pull the sheets off me and stumble out of the bedroom, making my way to the front door. There's another soft knock this time.

When I pull open the door, I'm surprised to see Devon standing there. The sun is just peeking up from behind him on the horizon. My brain isn't quite awake yet, but I'm already wondering what he's doing on my doorstep at the crack of dawn.

"Good morning, Sadie," he says, raising his eyebrows at me. I take a small step back as I realize how wild my hair must look. "I'm sorry to wake you. I tried your cell phone, but you didn't answer."

"Oh, no worries," I say, gesturing into the small space. "Come on in."

I instinctively cover my mouth just in case I have morning breath. As he walks in, I notice he's wearing a pair of fitted jeans, a white V-neck tee shirt, and a gray sweater. He looks great, as usual.

"I was actually wondering if you'd like to join me today. I have to drive to the coast to meet with one of our oyster suppliers."

"Really?" I perk up. I've always wanted to visit an oyster farm to see how the oysters are grown and harvested. It's like one of those Food Network episodes where viewers follow along at some famous chef shops for exclusive ingredients.

"Really. Can you be ready in a few minutes?" His eyes flit toward the espresso machine in the corner of the kitchen. "I'll make us some coffee."

"Yes, that'd be great. I'll be quick," I say as I practically skip back to the bedroom. I grab a pair of skinny jeans off the floor and pull on a blue sweater. A memory from the night before stops me as I slip on a pair of socks.

Norah and Luis kissing under the moonlight.

Does Devon know? I have a sick feeling in my stomach. Should I tell him?

I stumble over to the bathroom and look at myself in the mirror as I brush my teeth. It's not really my place to tell him, right? I mean, if he knew, what would happen to Thistle? I spit out the toothpaste and reach for my makeup bag.

As I put the last few strokes of mascara on my face, I decide to keep it professional today. There is no need for me to entangle myself in the personal lives of my bosses.

At least not yet.

When I step back into the kitchen, Devon has placed a small insulated coffee cup on the table for me. "Thanks," I say. I grab the cup and take a few sips. "Ready."

"Let's go," he says. I follow him out to the company van, which is white with the Thistle logo printed on the side. Like everything else here, it's new and top of the line. My thoughts wander to the fight I overheard between Devon and Luis the other night about money. Maybe Luis is right about spending too much money.

Devon takes a few long strides to step in front of me and opens the door. As I brush past him, I catch the faint smell of cologne. Not only does he look good, but he smells good too. What is Norah thinking?

"So where are we going today?" I ask as we settle into the front seat of the van.

Devon gives me a side smile. "East Maine Oyster Company. They have the best East Coast oysters in the United States. Greg, the owner, is going to meet us and give you a private tour. Then we have some business to discuss."

"Sounds good," I say, taking a sip of my coffee. Devon puts the car into drive, and we start angling down the driveway. In just a few minutes, we're on East-West Highway, heading toward the coast. I take my time sipping my coffee, which starts to clear the morning fog from my brain.

"So how do you like working at Thistle so far?" asks Devon.

"It's great," I say. "I mean, I hope I get to work in the kitchen a little bit more."

"I hope so too. I think you've got a lot of talent," he says with a small smile on his lips. "Everyone is treating you well?"

"Yes," I say. I put my coffee down in the cupholder. "Well, Norah is a little hard to figure out sometimes."

Devon makes a small grunting noise. "That's putting it nicely."

"I'm sure she's under a lot of pressure," I say. The last thing I want to do is talk bad about my boss's wife, especially when she's also my boss. Correction, my boss's *cheating* wife.

"She is," he says, looking out the window in a far-off way.

"Luis has been a big help, though. She's just too hard on herself."

I swallow. Yes, it looked like Luis was being very *helpful* last night. If we keep talking about Norah, I'm afraid I won't be able to stop myself from telling him what happened last night. I try to redirect the conversation.

"Thistle seems to be doing well," I offer.

He nods. "We're building a reputation. But it takes a while to be profitable."

Hence all the conversations about money I keep overhearing.

The truth is, I know very little about the business side of a restaurant. I feel like I have so much to learn as a chef that I've thought very little about how to make money. I just assumed all highly rated restaurants like Thistle were making more money than they know what to do with. They serve at least a few hundred reservations a week, and the checks average over seven hundred dollars per table. That has to add up over time.

"Was it hard to start over again after the fire at Pepper?"

He exhales. "Yes."

"It must have been really difficult to see your restaurant destroyed," I say. I can't help but bring it up after my conversation with Brian the other day. Was there really no insurance money? I know I can't ask Devon about it directly, but I'm still curious.

"It was very hard, but we managed to start over." I can tell he feels uncomfortable, but I push a little more.

"Did they ever find out how the fire started?"

Devon goes slightly stiff and remains silent. I'm afraid I've asked too much. But then he starts speaking again.

"It was an oven malfunction. Something with the starter," he says finally. "I really don't like to talk about it."

"Sorry," I say quietly. Devon says nothing and turns the car toward the exit.

"Hey, let's stop here and get a couple of croissant sandwiches for the road."

I'm grateful for the change of subject. And my stomach is growling. Devon has me wait in the van while he runs in to buy us breakfast. I watch him walk toward the door, the muscles in his back pressing against the jacket. He even looks good from behind.

I feel suddenly guilty for checking out my boss. But, geez, his wife is cheating on him, and he doesn't even know. That makes it somewhat less scandalous, right? I pull my fingers to my mouth, tempted to chew on my nails. A habit that Norah called me out on.

Why does she always have to be so mean? As I watch Devon walk back toward the van, a big smile on his face, I can't help but feel a bit sorry for him. Being married to Norah must be difficult.

He hops back in the van and hands me a warm ham and cheese croissant and a bottle of water.

"Breakfast is served, my lady," he says with a crooked smile.

"Thank you, sir," I say, picking up his playfulness. The two of us eat in silence for a while as we cruise down the road.

After breakfast, Devon begins to ask me about my life, where I'm from, and why I want to cook. I give him the highlights of the story about my dad. How he introduced me to farm-fresh food, and the diner we ran. Of course, I have to fudge a few of the details. I tell him I'm from Illinois instead of Ohio. And I leave out the part about heading to prison right after high school.

"So where's your Dad now?"

"He passed away a few years ago. While I was in school."

Telling that lie makes my stomach turn. The truth is much more difficult.

Dad passed while I was in prison. Throat cancer. It came on suddenly, a few months after I was locked away. When he got really sick, he couldn't visit me anymore. Even though I only served two years, he was gone by the time I was released. I never even made it to the funeral.

Part of me wishes I could open up to Devon about it. Instead, I swallow a lump in my throat and look out the window.

"Oh, I'm so sorry," he says. He reaches over and places a hand on top of mine. "And your mom?"

"She died when I was little."

"Wow, I'm sorry, Sadie."

I shrug my shoulders, and he puts his hand back on the steering wheel. "It's just me, but I've gotten used to it. I've learned the best person to rely on is yourself."

"You are wise beyond your years," he says. His compliment cheers me up a little.

"What about you? Are you still in touch with your parents?"

"Sadly, no," he says. "My parents also passed away when I was young. In college, actually. I drifted around for a while and ended up in New York. That's when I met Norah."

Again, Norah is the last topic I want to discuss right now. "What about the Winthrop estate? Did your parents leave that to you?"

"Sort of. It's in a trust, actually. When my parents passed, I became the beneficiary, so the farm became mine."

"Any brothers or sisters?"

"No."

I tuck my hand under my chin. Devon and I have a lot more in common than I thought. Both of us orphaned as young adults. No siblings. I'm sure it wasn't easy for him. It certainly wasn't easy for me.

We fall silent for a moment, just a bit of music on the radio and the hum of the van. My thoughts drift back to last night in the restaurant. When I thought I heard a familiar name.

Samantha. It's been years since someone has called me by that name. Five years exactly.

In many ways, Samantha was a completely different person. But she was also me.

Even though I do everything I can to push away the past, memories of that night rush back to me. I was only eighteen years old when the cops slapped the cold steel handcuffs on my wrists. I didn't cry. I could only stare at the ground. I wasn't sure exactly what to say or do in that moment. All I could think about was the sight of my best friend. Her sparkly green eyes, now cold and staring off into the distance. The feel of her cold skin as I reached out to touch her.

I take a few deep breaths, trying to exhale the past. I push the thoughts back down into my brain, telling myself I'll deal with those things later. I spent plenty of time thinking about that night in prison. The only thing I need to think about now is the future.

I see a sign along the highway for East Maine Oyster

Company, which snaps me out of my thoughts of the past. Devon turns off the road.

"We're here," he says. "You ready to do some fresh oyster tasting?"

"Absolutely," I say.

The time in the car has allowed me to get to know Devon a little bit more. And so far, I really like what I know. And the more time I spend with him, the more guilty I feel for not telling him about Norah and Luis.

But if there's one thing I've learned about revealing secrets, it's this—timing is everything.

15

Devon rolls down the window, and the smell of the ocean drifts into the car. The road changes from pavement to gravel, and I can hear the crunch of the tires underneath as we make our way to the coastline.

We climb out of the car and walk toward a charming clapboard building with a well-manicured yard and large sign out front. Greg is waiting for us by the edge of the gravel parking lot. He's a large man, probably six feet two, with a full beard and a deep voice.

"Devon," he says with a nod.

"Greg," Devon says, stopping a few feet in front of him. "Thanks for seeing me on short notice."

Greg gives him a tight smile. "You didn't give me much of a choice."

Devon gestures toward me. "This is Sadie; she's a new member of our kitchen staff. I was hoping you could show her the oyster cages and teach her a little bit about how your farm works."

Greg eyes me up and down. I step forward and offer my hand. "Nice to meet you, Greg."

He doesn't take my hand, so for a few seconds it stays suspended in the air between us. I finally drop my hand.

Awkward.

"Likewise," he says. His posture is stiff, like he feels uncomfortable around us. "I've got the boat ready in the back. I can take the two of you out, and then Devon and I can discuss some business."

"Sounds perfect," Devon says. Greg turns and heads down toward the dock. I was expecting some friendly banter between the two men, but instead we walk in silence.

When we arrive at the docks behind the building, Greg hands me a pair of waders and a thick life jacket, which I slip into immediately. I'm not a huge fan of water. The three of us step onto a long aluminum boat. Greg is up front in the cabin while Devon and I sit on a bench in the back.

The oyster cages are spread out across the water in a large loop. We make our way around them while Greg explains the types of oysters they produce. Devon asks him questions about the flavor profile, size, and acidity. I chide myself for not bringing my notebook; otherwise I would be feverishly taking notes.

I breathe in the crisp fall air, letting it settle into my lungs, and relax my body as we motor around the water. Just as we're making our way around the last few oyster cages, I feel my phone buzz in my pocket. I ignore the message and lean in to listen to Greg explain something about spring cleaning the oysters. My phone buzzes again. Devon gets up from his seat next to me to stand with Greg at the front of the boat.

I reluctantly pull out my phone and swipe it open. I find

a series of text messages from Sally. Suddenly, I remember her message from last night. I was so exhausted that I forgot to call her back. I read her messages.

> Sadie, you need to call me.

> There's a man who keeps coming into the diner looking for you.

And the last message she wrote makes the floor drop out of my stomach.

> He's asking for Samantha.

"Is everything okay?" Devon is standing over me. I quickly stash my phone back in my bag.

"It's fine," I say, brushing some of the curls out of my face. "Just an old friend I used to work with."

"Oh," he says, a slight frown crinkling his brow. "Well, come up to the front of the boat. Greg wants to show us the current crop."

"Right," I say.

I try to listen as Greg points out which oysters are in their second year and which are ready for harvest, but all I can think of is Sally's message. Who would be looking for Samantha? I know I made some mistakes, but I've served my time for what I did.

Prison wasn't easy—erratic sleep mixed with either extreme stress or extreme boredom. And just thinking about the bland food makes my stomach flip. I thought I put all of that behind me. I served my time, and I don't owe anything to anyone.

I listen politely as Greg guides us back to the oyster farm

headquarters, but I'm itching to text Sally back. As soon as we pull into the dock, I hop off the boat and excuse myself to go to the bathroom. I pull out my phone and type a message.

I can't talk right now. Can I come by the diner tomorrow morning?

I wait a few minutes, which feels like an eternity. Then I see the message bubbles appear.

Yup, I'll be here.

Thanks.

I stash my phone back in my bag and wash my hands. As I step out of the bathroom, I peer around the corner. Devon and Greg are outside the building, talking. They don't look happy. And something tells me not to interrupt.

"You promised me, Greg," Devon says.

Greg raises his hands. "Hey, man, I've got other customers," he says.

"Is this about Naomi? Did she call you?"

I step closer to the window, keeping my back up against the wall so they can't see me. *Who's Naomi?*

"No," Greg says. "And whatever you two are doing over there at Thistle, I want no part of it. I know who loaned you the money, Devon. And I want nothing to do with them."

"Too late, you're already involved. It only takes one phone call and you'll have some not-so-friendly visitors at your door."

Greg takes a step toward Devon, towering over him. "Are you threatening me?"

I can't believe what I'm hearing. Is this how Devon does business with all his vendors? Fearing that the two of them might actually get into a fistfight, I decide to step in. I take a few strides and rip open the door.

"Hey, guys, thanks for waiting on me."

The two of them take a step back from each other. There's a brief moment of awkward silence as the three of us stand in a semicircle.

"It's time for us to get back to the restaurant." Devon breaks the silence, looking at me and then Greg. "Would you like to help us load up the van?"

Greg glares at Devon. For a moment, I think he might say no. He scrapes his beard with his fingers. "Sure," he says.

I help Greg and Devon load a half a dozen cases of oysters into the van. The cases are heavy with ice, and the three of us work in a tense silence. Once we're packed up and on the road, I breathe a small sigh of relief. I definitely didn't get the feeling we were welcome at East Maine Oyster Company.

"So what did you think, Sadie, pretty cool, right?" Devon seems pretty upbeat for a guy who just about got into a fistfight with his supplier.

"Very cool," I say. "Have you worked with Greg for long?"

He nods. "He used to supply oysters for us back at Pepper. In fact, I put his oyster company on the map. Now every high-end restaurant from here to California wants to work with him. Sometimes it's hard to stay first in line for the best oysters on the East Coast."

I can see that.

I guess I can't blame Devon for threatening him. They seem to have known each other for a while. But why would Greg not want to work with Devon? Who is Devon in business with that seems to make Greg not want to supply oysters for Thistle?

"So tell me, Sadie, if Thistle were your restaurant, how would you do the menu?"

"Me?" All thoughts of the oyster farm suddenly vanish, replaced with a flood of ideas I've been dying to share. "Well, I'd start with an amuse-bouche of..."

I walk Devon through an entire menu. There have been many nights—whether I was sleeping in my car or sitting in the cabin kitchen after a long shift—where I've sat down and made notes on my dream menu.

We banter back and forth about food ingredients the rest of the way home. He asks me questions, like *what if we had a delivery of lamb? Or pork? What if you run out of something we have on the menu?*

For me, it's a fun "what-if" type of conversation. But it also feels like an interview.

After he drops me off at the cabin, the high of discussing my fictional menu falls away, and I'm left with a bit of dread. Not only do I have to meet Sally tomorrow at the diner, but I also have the uncomfortable sensation that I might be getting too close to something that's going on at Thistle.

Something that might get me sent back to jail.

16

The next morning, I make my way to Mike's Diner. Not able to find a spot beside the semis and work trucks, I pull my car onto the grass lot next to the highway.

I step into the busy diner and am hit by the smell of burnt bacon. A man sitting at the table by the door has turned his sausages, biscuits, and scrambled eggs into soup by pouring a bucketful of gravy over everything. But I remember the smells and the preschool art fair presentation of food—the shock is in the noise. The kitchen sizzles and beeps as Mike shouts, the customers holler across the room at each other, the TV on the edge of the counter blares, and a new truck pulls into the lot and yanks on its horn.

I eye the row of chairs in front of the counter before spotting a round pleather seat. It's the only one that isn't punctured by keys or doesn't wobble when you sit down. Sally's at the far corner of the counter, serving coffee. She's wearing her blue uniform apron, her hair piled in a messy bun on top of her head with a pencil sticking out the back.

"Sally," I say. She nods in my direction and makes her way down the line.

"Hey, Sadie," she says before dropping a ceramic mug in front of me and filling it with coffee. "Give me a few minutes, and then let's chat out back, okay?"

I accept the coffee, which despite looking like motor-oil sludge, doesn't taste too bad. It's definitely not as good as the espresso I make in my little cabin. I let the steam warm my cheeks and try to keep my face turned away from the customers. The last thing I'm looking for is a reunion with my old customers.

In some ways, Mike's reminds me of my dad's place. Our diner was set in the downtown area of a small town in Ohio. It was the main morning stop for everyone who lived there, from businessmen to farmers. Dad was a great cook; he focused on fresh ingredients and minimized the use of the fryer. Although, fried food couldn't be totally done away with, or the customers might have gone on strike.

When I see Sally nod toward the door, I drain the last of my coffee. I make my way to the exit and walk around the diner building. Sally is smoking a cigarette by the dumpster.

"You know you should kick the habit, right?"

She rolls her eyes. "I know, I know." She takes a long puff and tosses the cigarette on the ground, then snuffs it out with her tennis shoe. "Glad you came by, kid."

"Glad you called," I reply.

"I've got something for you," she says as she digs her hand into her apron. She pulls out the black leather pad she uses to take orders and slips out a small business card. She hands it to me.

"This is his card. Said his name is Carl."

I look down at the card in my hand, white with black and

red letters. It reads *Carl Smithfield, Private Investigator* and then has a phone number. The private investigator part makes me wince.

"He told me to call him if I saw or heard of anyone named Samantha Reynolds. He was given a tip she was living in this area."

I stare at the card. "Did he say how he found Mike's?"

Sally shakes her head. "No. Just asked if I knew Samantha. And showed me a picture of you with red hair and green feather earrings."

I raise my eyes and meet hers. "That was a long time ago."

"Yeah, I figured it was. The girl in the photo was very young. Maybe eighteen."

I think of the day that photo was taken. I remember because my best friend, Erica, spent the night at my house the night before. We bought a box of hair dye at the local pharmacy, and the result was a copper style that I wore for my senior picture. We planned to get up early to do our makeup and hair together. But it didn't exactly happen that way.

We stayed up way too late doing a scary movie marathon —from *Scream* to *Saw*—and neither of us could sleep. I remember laughing until I practically peed my pants the next morning when she suggested we dunk our heads in ice water to get rid of the bags under our eyes. Which actually worked. We both looked fresh and awake for the photos despite our severe lack of sleep. She insisted I wear her new feather earrings.

That was all *before* the accident.

"What did you tell him?" I ask.

"Nothing," she says. "Absolutely nothing. You served your time, kiddo. You don't owe anybody anything."

Sally's words bring back the memories of that night. I try to push them away, but as I blink, I see the deer, the shattered glass and the blood. It was an accident. But if I hadn't been drinking...I shake my head, pushing down the familiar tug of guilt.

When I was sentenced to prison, I felt like I deserved it. The guilt is something I will have to live with for the rest of my life. I thought maybe serving time in prison would alleviate some of that dull, anxious feeling, but it continues to follow me like a dark cloud chasing my every last step.

And now someone is looking for me. *Or at least, the old me.*

Sally is watching me as I stare at the card. I reach out and give her a quick hug, the cheap perfume enveloping me in Sally's warmth.

"I have to get to work," I say, pulling away. "Thanks for covering for me."

"No sweat, kid," she says.

I turn and walk back to my car, my feet crunching loudly over the gravel parking lot. I'm sure other people have been through worse than I have, more tragedy, more loss. Sometimes it's all I can do to put one foot in front of the other.

But I try not to think about what's behind me. That's all in the past.

17

I keep my head down for the next few days, trying to keep my mind focused on my present...and not my past. When I arrive for Thursday's shift, I'm relieved to find Luis waiting by the back door of the kitchen with a white apron in his hand—not a server uniform. I breathe a sigh of relief, assuming my post at the dishwashing station has been reinstated. I can't risk being seen in the front of the restaurant again.

Given the exclusivity of Thistle, whoever is looking for me will have a hard time getting a reservation here. So even if I have to wait tables again, it's unlikely that some private investigator would be able to get a table. At least, that's what I tell myself as I tie on the bleached white apron.

I'm so preoccupied with thoughts from my meeting with Sally this morning that I barely notice when Luis walks me over to the food prep station and hands me a knife. Then it occurs to me—I might not be washing dishes tonight.

"Am I cooking?" I ask tenuously.

He smiles, nods. "Tonight you'll be working with our pastry chef, Charlie," he says.

"And Norah is okay with this?"

My memory flickers back to her comment that I belong in the dining room.

He shrugs. "It wasn't completely up to her." Charlie steps into view, his white chef's coat looking freshly washed and with a slight fold at the collar. "Chef, this is Sadie."

"We've met," he says.

"Great," Luis says. One of the other cooks shouts his name near the ovens. "I'll leave you two to work."

Luis turns and quickly walks away. I'm left standing in front of a large stainless-steel table with a cutting board in front of me. Charlie turns around and pulls out a large strainer of bright red strawberries. There must be at least five pounds of berries in the bowl.

"You ready?" asks Charlie.

"Yes, chef," I say, forcefully brushing away any thoughts of the past.

"Minced, please," he says and walks to the other end of the table.

I take a deep breath and pour a mound of strawberries out in front of me. I feel a few butterflies in my stomach as I begin cutting into the juicy red berries. Part of me is pinching myself; I am actually working as a cook in a Michelin-starred restaurant.

My dad would be so proud.

As I set to work, I also hear the voice of Professor Chang, who taught knife skills at CIA. She was a petite woman with jet-black hair. Despite her size, she was very intimidating and would not hesitate to correct her students with a biting word. "A rocking motion with the knife, Sadie!" she would say. "You are not chopping wood with an axe."

By the time I finish all five pounds of strawberries, I'm sweating inside my white tunic. Charlie returns to my side with a fresh-baked tray of donuts. The sweet, sugary smell is intoxicating. I'm too afraid to ask him what dish we're working on, but I'm already intrigued.

As if reading my mind, Charlie says, "Tonight's dessert is strawberries and basil cream malassada with a honey crisp." He reaches over and drops a large bundle of basil leaves in front of me. "Chiffonade, please, no bruising."

I know this cutting technique, although I might be a bit rusty. Charlie works alongside me as I roll the basil up like a small joint and carefully slice the leaves. Meanwhile, he cuts each donut precisely in half. Rows and rows of doughy pastry cut perfectly in half. Once we have both finished, I stand and wait as he drops the strawberries in small batches into a large bowl of freshly whipped cream. He folds them in carefully and slowly, as if he's defusing a bomb.

Next we create the honey crisp. This requires a double boiler and a candy thermometer to heat the honey to a precise temp. Charlie then carefully pours out the honey onto a sheet, shapes it, and uses a ruler to create the right thickness.

"Sadie, come," he says, pointing to the empty space next to him. "Now we will plate this dish. Place the plates in rows. We will put the pastries two inches from the edge of the plate on two sides, like this."

He places one of the sliced pastries at the corner of the plate. He then pulls out a small stainless-steel ruler and measures exactly two inches. With precise artistry, Charlie assembles the dish carefully. Fried pastry, strawberry-laced cream, a finely set honey crisp. A delicately placed basil leaf on the corner.

If I had my phone on me, I would snap a photo, although it would be wholly inappropriate. Although he's silent, I can no longer hold in my admiration.

"This is amazing, how did you think of this?"

He cocks one eyebrow, gives me a side look. "Not me. Norah. She is the genius behind all the dishes here."

Of course, Norah.

I feel myself bubble up with a new sense of respect. The presentation, the combination of fresh ingredients—it's pure genius. I have a long way to go before I can create at the level of the renowned Mrs. Winthrop.

When I was washing dishes, I mostly had my back to the kitchen and a view out the window. But now that I'm working with Charlie, I have a full view of all the stations around the large room. I try to absorb everything I see, from the posture of the staff to the interactions between the cooks.

I notice Luis and Norah are side by side nearly the entire night. Norah seems like a different person around him. Her facial expressions are softer. She smiles more. I even see her drop her head back and laugh at one point. Now that I know the two of them are having an affair, I wonder how I missed it before. It's obvious, but I just wasn't paying attention.

I've never seen her smile at Devon, not once. As soon as he walks into the room, she stiffens and makes herself busy. I bite my lip as I continue working. *What happened between the two of them?*

I shake my head. It's really none of my business.

As if on cue, I see Norah approaching from the back of the kitchen. She tips her chin at Charlie's creation, taking a moment to adjust a few of the honey crisps.

"Adjust the angle of the crisps, like this," she says, moving the corner slightly. "And where is the strawberry caviar?"

"Oh, I'm sorry!" Charlie says. "Just a moment and I'll pull them from the refrigerator."

Charlie steps over to the large glass-front refrigerator and pulls out a bowl of water with tiny red caviar beads inside.

"I made these this morning," he says.

With a large pair of tweezers, Norah plucks a few beads of red caviar and places them on the dish. I watch her intently, standing back far enough to not be noticed. As she stretches her arm across the table, her sleeve slides back. I notice a few marks that look like bruises.

They're in the same pattern as the ones she had the day we met. I steal a glance at Charlie. He looks away, not making eye contact. I know he saw them as well. Norah pulls her sleeve back down.

"Wonderful work, chef. Thank you," Norah says. Just as she's about to walk away, she turns in my direction. I give a quick smile and nod. She looks me up and down in response and walks away.

I wonder if she even wanted me to work in the kitchen at all. She seems happier when I'm scrubbing burnt pans in the sink, a job that's been thankfully taken over by a new hire. Norah's difficult to read, but from what I can tell so far, she's hard to impress.

Charlie finishes his work, perfectly replicating the composition she created. As I watch food runners retrieve the plates and carry them out to the dining room, I feel a renewed sense of purpose. There's just so much for me to learn here at Thistle. I must find a way to stay longer.

And let's face it. If I leave now, my prospects for a new job are pretty slim. There's a seven-year look-back period for felonies in Maine, so I'm just two years away from a clean record. After that, my options are wide open.

"We'll load the rest of the malassada into the cooler until the servers need them," Charlie says as he picks up one of the trays. I follow suit, carefully picking up a tray and walking behind him. We're just a few steps from the larger walk-in cooler when one of the hostesses approaches me.

"Sadie, I'm glad I found you," she says, walking alongside me. "One of the guests has requested you stop by the table."

I feel my stomach drop, and at the same time, I stumble, nearly dropping six plates of the carefully designed malassada.

"Sorry!" I say. Charlie drops off his tray at one of the nearby stations, turns to me and pulls the tray from my hands.

"More careful next time," he says with a stern look.

"This way, Sadie," says the hostess. I feel my cheeks burn as I follow her, and my mind spins. If someone is out there looking for Samantha, I have zero chance of getting away. Which means all the progress I've made here at Thistle is going to be thrown out with the trash. I will be forced to leave.

As she leads me deeper into the dining room, my mind swirls with possibilities. Should I pretend to be sick? Make a run for the bathroom? The customers are king at Thistle; not following this hostess could mean my job regardless.

But why is someone looking for me? Both my parents are gone.

What could someone want from Samantha Reynolds?

To me, she's as good as dead.

18

Leaving the kitchen and entering the dining room is like passing from one world to another. The sounds of pots and pans banging around, the sharp click of knives against cutting boards, and the hiss of the steam from the ovens give way to the conversational rhythm of a Friday night dinner service.

I search the room for any type of familiar face while trying not to appear like I am eavesdropping on people. The hostess charges ahead without looking back at me as she makes her way to the corner of the room. I can figure out a way to save my job with the Winthrops later.

The hostess arrives at a table, and I instantly let out the breath I've been holding. It's the couple from the other night who ordered the two-inch ice cubes. The woman's eyes light up as she sees me.

What were their names? Gristle? Griswald? Goris?

"Sadie! We were hoping you might help us. You know that ice you found for us the other night?"

Come on, remember! Oh yes...

"Mr. and Mrs. Grissom, of course I can help," I say, feeling a wave of relief hit my body. The beaming expressions on their faces confirm I remembered their name correctly.

"Oh, Sadie, that's wonderful. You see, my husband likes his old-fashioned with a two-inch ice cube..."

I assure them I can help. And after a quick scan around the room, I realize no one else is looking for me. The hostess who pulled me out of the kitchen has already left the table. I finally exhale, feeling all the tension leave my body.

After I have helped the Grissoms with their ice request, I march back to the kitchen. I'm not sure who was serving their table tonight, not to mention how they got a second reservation, but I am grateful it was them and not someone else.

I bounce back to the dessert station with a renewed sense of hope. Maybe this will work out after all. When I see who's waiting for me, I stop cold.

"Sadie, where have you been?" Norah asks.

"A guest requested me at their table. For ice," I say. Surely, she'll understand.

"You are not to leave your station. It is not your job to serve ice to the guests. I've been working with Charlie to pick up the slack," she says as she dices some pears. Charlie keeps his head down, setting out plates with a small collection of chocolates on them.

"I'm sorry," I offer.

"I want you to finish dicing these pears, clean the entire station top to bottom, and then help Oscar polish the silverware." She glares at me again.

"I'm sorry, I—"

She holds her palm up in my face, then raises her voice.

"Another mistake like this and you'll be back at Mike's Diner."

She turns on her heel and walks to the other side of the room. The words "Mike's Diner" practically echo off the wall. A few cooks look up from their stations in my direction. I feel my cheeks burn. Not only was her scolding over the top, but she's made it a point to embarrass me in front of all the kitchen staff.

A knot forms in my throat, which I swallow. Why did she have to bring *that* up? My cheeks continue to burn as I get back to work.

Why do I let her get under my skin? I've been to prison, for goodness' sake; I can handle a little scolding from Norah. But it still hurts a little. I mean, she practically made a formal announcement that my last job was working at a diner. I feel like I need to shout out how many credits I've already earned from CIA. But I never finished, so what would be the point?

I turn my focus to chopping pears, not daring to look up for a moment.

A few minutes later, Devon appears in the kitchen. I dare a glance in his direction when I hear him greet the staff. He looks dashing, wearing a black suit with a white button-down and no tie. The slight opening at the collar shows off the top of his tan chest. He scans the room and sets his eyes on Norah.

I watch as he approaches her. She's speaking with one of the cooks at the meat station. He taps her lightly on the arm. She spins around.

He leans in and speaks softly in her ear. Her eyes go wide; then she slams her hand on the table.

"What do you mean they don't like it?" she screams. All

the sound of cooking in the room stops for a moment. It's as if a giant vacuum has sucked the air out of the room.

"Norah, keep your voice down," he says.

"Keep my voice down? I am so sick of you telling me what to do, Devon." She begins pulling at the strings on her apron. "This just isn't going to work anymore. I can't be something I'm not."

Devon reaches for Norah's bicep and squeezes. "Not here."

Norah takes a step back. "Don't touch me."

She finishes taking off her apron and shoves it into his chest, then turns and storms across the room and out the back door. Luis, who was working at a station nearby, calls after her. She doesn't look back. He follows her out the door.

Devon stands for a moment in silence, watching her walk out of the room. His face turns bright red. Now it's his turn to be humiliated by Norah. The apron sticks to his chest for a few seconds, then falls to the floor. Everyone seems frozen at their stations, wondering what to do next. Thistle is Norah's brainchild, her culinary genius at work. If she's gone, what are the rest of us supposed to do?

Devon straightens the front of his jacket and shifts his jaw.

"Back to work, everyone," he says as he looks around, a tight smile on his lips. It looks like he might follow Norah and Luis out the back door for a moment. But instead, he turns and walks back into the dining room.

I finish dicing the pears and offer them to Charlie. He doesn't speak much for the rest of the night. After I've polished and scrubbed every surface of our workstation, I head to the storage room to polish silverware with Oscar. When I arrive, Ingrid informs me that Oscar was sent home early—by Norah, I'm sure—and I'm left polishing over one hundred pieces of silverware by myself.

By the time I arrive back at my cabin, it's past midnight. I peel off my clothes, turn out the lights, and crawl into bed. I lie there thinking about what happened in the kitchen tonight. Norah seems to be fed up with Devon. She seems to be on the verge of quitting her position as head chef. And if she does leave, what does that mean for Thistle?

I mean, Norah is difficult to work with, yes, but I was just starting to make my way up the kitchen ladder. I'm finally getting the kitchen experience I need to move my career forward. Devon doesn't seem like someone who would give up so easily, but from what I know, it's always been the two of them working together. I'm not sure how Devon would pull this off on his own.

This is one of those times I desperately wish I could call my dad for advice. The two of us cooking in the kitchen together is the last thing I think of before falling asleep.

19

The next morning, I report to the kitchen at my normal hour. I'm not sure what to expect when I walk in, given that Norah charged out of the kitchen last night without looking back. So I'm a bit surprised to see everyone at their usual stations, prepping for tonight's reservations.

It's as if the whole scene Norah made last night about quitting didn't even happen. I guess, given her volatile personality, it wouldn't surprise me if she's done this before.

I make my way to the dessert station. Charlie hasn't arrived yet, but I see a couple of piles of fresh fruit lying on the stainless-steel workstation. Without knowing what's on the menu for this evening, I'm not sure where to start.

"Good morning, Sadie."

I turn to see Devon walking up to my station. He looks a bit bedraggled; his normal five-o'clock shadow has almost grown into a beard overnight. He's wearing the same clothes as last night.

"Hi, Devon, what's up?" I ask, trying to sound casual. Like

I didn't see Norah humiliate him in front of all the kitchen staff last night.

"Can we talk?" he asks. "In my office?"

"Sure."

I've never been to his office before, but I know it's out the side entrance of the building, down the path. The building was an old milk house and, as part of the renovations of the property, was converted into an office.

He opens the door for me, and we walk inside. The office is one large room with a collection of windows wrapping around the sides. Cherrywood paneling covers the floor, walls, and ceiling. I don't know much about interior design, but I'm sure the wood paneling alone cost a fortune. Devon's desk sits in the center of the room below large glass skylights.

"Have a seat," he says, gesturing to one of the leather chairs across from his desk.

"Everything okay?" I say as he takes a seat across from me.

He looks up at me, his blue eyes slightly cloudy. "No, it's not." He takes a deep breath. "Charlie has quit on me," he says.

"Wow, I'm sorry to hear that," I say. I am sorry. But I also see an opportunity. If Charlie is gone, then...

"Me too. He made it clear he's not coming back into work tonight. Or ever."

I rub the side of my neck. Of course I want to know more, but Devon seems so frazzled I don't want to press for details. He brushes his hand through his thick auburn hair. Even with little sleep, and the stress wearing on his face, he's still handsome. I finger the sides of the paper coffee cup he's given me as I try to come up with the appropriate response.

"What happened?"

"I don't know. He called me and left a message on my phone. Said something about him being too old to work in such a negative work environment. Maybe Norah got to him." He shakes his head and looks out the window. "Did he seem upset last night?"

I flip through my memories of the night, checking to make sure it had nothing to do with me. I remember Charlie being a little frustrated when I nearly dropped the tray of perfectly arranged desserts, but other than that, he seemed normal.

"I can't think of anything. Norah had him tweak some dishes, but he didn't seem upset at the time."

Devon leans back in his chair. "Well, something happened," he says. "And Norah can be difficult."

I'm afraid to say anything, but of course I agree. "I'm sure she's under a lot of pressure."

"She wasn't always like this." He sighs. "And now I'm one cook short in the kitchen. The timing can't be worse."

"Why is that?"

He looks at me with an intense look in his eyes. "I've heard rumors we're up for a second Michelin star. They never formally announce anything until the review is complete. But one of my former colleagues informed me a Michelin inspector was here last week."

Ripples of excitement spread through my stomach. A second Michelin star. Just the idea of having a hand in a restaurant that has earned the coveted honor makes my stomach flip-flop.

"That's amazing, Devon. I'm sure you'll get the star. The menu and service at Thistle is top-notch."

He takes a small sip of his coffee and shifts in his seat. "I hope so. And it's why I'm here. I need your help."

"Me? I mean, yeah, of course. What can I help with?"

He turns, and his eyes latch on to me so deeply I'm afraid to blink. "I need you to take his place. As lead on the pastry station."

I feel my heart skip at least three beats. "As pastry chef?"

"Yes," says Devon.

I take a sip of coffee. *Is this too good to be true?*

"Are you sure? I mean, I only worked with Charlie one night. And I haven't even finished CIA—"

"After the way you cooked for me the other night? You've got the talent, Sadie. It's the same kind of *it* factor that Norah had when she first started out. You've got something I haven't seen another chef possess in years. The creativity with the dishes, the flavor profiles. And that's just the one time you cooked for me. I can only imagine what else you're capable of. I know you can do this."

I feel myself blush. This is definitely not how I expected my morning to go. I'm trying to catch my bearings. Devon has just made me an incredible offer. But I can't help but feel like I don't deserve it. *Does he really think I have that kind of talent?*

Regardless, it's an offer that every classmate at CIA would have literally salivated at.

I take a deep breath.

"I can help you," I say, training my eye on Devon's facial expressions, "but I'd like to create at least one of my own dishes—a caramel apple tarte, maybe. And I want it on the menu, next to Norah's."

He looks at me, a touch of surprise in his expression. "Okay, but Norah—"

"You'll have to convince her," I say, trying to sound firm. He rubs the stubble on his chin, studying my face. Then he shrugs.

"Done," he says. "Anything else?"

Should I have asked for more? I feel a twist in my stomach. My brain spins.

"Yes, and a promise," I say, folding my lips into my mouth and back. "That you'll back me with a referral when I open my own restaurant."

I watch carefully as Devon responds to my request. He leans back in his chair and brushes the back of his fingers along his face.

"I'll let you create your own dishes," he says. "But you'll have to earn a referral if you want in in my investor network." A little smile plays at the edge of his lips. "And you have to finish the year here at Thistle."

I mirror his smile. *Finish the year?* I would stay two years if I'm able to head the pastry station. A tingling sensation spreads through my chest. There's so much I can learn from this. And it's just the experience I've been looking for. Even if I'm not ready to start my own restaurant, Devon's referral could get me a job anywhere I want.

As long as they don't dig too far into my past.

"It's a deal." I hold out my hand.

He grasps my hand in his. For a moment, our eyes meet. I feel a little spark run up my arm. We suspend our hands over the desk for a moment before Devon pulls his hand away and reaches down to his briefcase.

"Well, Sadie, you have some work to do," he says. He pulls out a stack of laminated cards. There are recipes and photos on each card. I'm guessing this is Norah's handiwork. And I know it will be my job to bring each dish to life.

As he places them on the table, I reach eagerly across the table to retrieve them. My heart is beating so fast it may well burst out of my chest. This is it. I've been waiting for this moment since the day I sliced the pages from the magazine in Barnes and Noble.

I lose track of time for a moment, my fingers grazing across each laminated sheet, studying the recipes. My eyes soak in each ingredient and dish. Sheep's milk mousse, steamed chocolate sponge with baked white chocolate, and sugar snap salad. They all sound incredible. As I salivate over each dish, I can feel Devon's eyes on me.

"These look incredible," I say, feeling my brain light up with ideas.

We make eye contact for a moment. I want to tell him he's just made all my dreams come true. But I'm afraid if I do, he might recant his offer. So I just smile.

"Thank you," I say.

"No, thank you, Sadie," he says. He reaches down and gathers up his leather briefcase and coffee. "I'll see you tonight. Have fun learning from Norah."

I swallow hard, already picturing the disappointment on her face. All I can do is nod. I get up and head for the door, grasping the glossy photos of food close to my chest as I walk back to the kitchen. I need to be ready to mimic every detail of the arrangement, just like Charlie did for Norah.

It's just all happening so *fast.*

Of course, I'm thrilled that I'll actually be acting as chef tonight, but something keeps pulling at the back of my brain. Like, why me? Why was I thrust into this opportunity and not one of the other cooks? It just feels like there's something I might be missing.

At this point, it doesn't matter. I know that things at

Thistle aren't perfect. But I don't need them to be perfect to take what experience I need and move forward. Devon seems to be impressed with my work so far, but Norah is going to be much harder to please.

And if she isn't happy? I have some ideas that might change her mind.

20

I arrive back in the kitchen with a renewed sense of purpose. I weave my way through people carrying crates and boxes full of food. I can already smell a combination of rising yeast and the earth from the fresh vegetables. Vendors are coming and going, Luis greeting them and signing for packages.

I pass him and head to the room where the uniforms are kept. I'm too nervous to say hello and ask him any questions, of which I'm sure there will be plenty. Avoiding Norah's wrath is probably impossible, but I've already decided that I will go to Luis with my questions.

I step up to the rack of uniforms and pull out a white chef's jacket. I run my hands over the starched white cotton before slipping it on. It fits me snugly, and I can't help feel a little jolt of excitement at the prospect of being a real chef. Dad would have been so proud of me.

I head back to the dessert station, which is already stacked with the fresh ingredients we'll be using tonight. We have strawberries again, some fresh herbs, citrus fruits from the greenhouse, and a few bushels of apples. The ingredients seem fairly basic and simple, but I know with Norah's recipes I'll be able to create something unique. I take inventory of everything in front of me and select a few recipes to work with.

Once I have a plan in my head of exactly how I will make her dishes, I sketch out a recipe of my own.

The kitchen meeting starts in fifteen minutes. I look up only when Norah comes in through the back door. Her expression is dark, but the rest of her looks neatly pressed and ready to work. She makes a beeline for Luis. Her face softens as she makes eye contact with him. He greets her warmly and places his hand on her back.

I watch as the two of them talk quietly in the corner. It's a little disgusting, really. They're not really hiding the affair at all. I mean, their body language makes it obvious they are more than just coworkers. My thoughts go back to Peter and the chef's wife at Château Bernard. The situation is so similar. Except here I have much more to lose. I'm not just a waitress anymore.

I shake my head. It's probably better to bury the scene I witnessed the other night and pretend I never saw them. But it does make me look at Devon a bit differently.

Again, probably not a good idea.

I turn my attention back to my notes. There are plenty of things for me to worry about over the next ten hours. The personal lives of my bosses is not one of them.

"Meeting!" Luis calls out to the kitchen staff. Almost every person in the room lines up like a group of schoolkids as we make our way to the dining room. A long table is already set for us with water and a pile of fresh croissants. I have heard Luis say before that he can't think on an empty stomach. Norah, on the other hand, looks as if she hasn't eaten enough for months.

Once everyone has settled in their seats, Luis starts the meeting.

"Good morning, everyone," he says after taking a sip of water. "I'm sure some of you have heard the buzz that we may or may not have had a special visitor last week from Michelin."

A few murmurs float up around the table.

"Word on the street is that we are up for a second Michelin star. And there may be an inspector coming tonight. So execution is important. Everything must be perfect," he says. "Let's go around the table and discuss dishes for each course."

Each chef takes turns discussing their dishes for the evening. Luis offers feedback on each dish, then turns to Norah for a final nod of approval. To my surprise, she barely speaks for the entire meeting. She really just stares straight ahead, her expression neutral and unreadable. I can only imagine what types of thoughts must be going through her mind. Luis, in general, seems to be running the show.

"Sadie, what do you have for us?" Luis calls on me.

I feel all the blood drain from my limbs as I straighten up in my seat.

"I reviewed the recipes from Norah this morning," I say, looking toward Norah. "And with the fresh ingredients we have, I'm thinking of macerated strawberries with a yogurt parfait and pistachio crumble."

Luis is smiling at me while I talk, which I take as a bit of encouragement. Norah's facial expression remains completely unreadable. I clear my throat.

"And for the apples, I have a recipe of my own I want to share if that's okay?"

All the faces at the table shift from me to Norah. She remains perfectly still.

"Go ahead," says Luis.

"Well, we have some fresh Vermont apples, which have a balanced sweet-tart flavor. So I'd like to create a caramelized puff pastry, layered with warm cinnamon baked apples, a crème pâtissière with caramel piped in between the layers. Then I would like to top it with quenelle of cinnamon- and rosemary-infused ice cream."

I hold up a quick sketch of the dish. Every eye at the table is trained on me. I set the sketch down and fumble with the collar of my chef's jacket.

Have I overstepped my place on my first day? Maybe I am asking for too much. Luis leans over and speaks quietly in Norah's ear. She leans in to listen, keeping her eyes trained on me as he speaks.

Finally, she straightens in her seat. Time stretches out like taffy as I wait for her response.

"Let's try it," she says. "But I'll need to taste it before dinner service. Also—" She cocks her head to the side. "Leave out the cinnamon in the ice cream. It may overpower the dish."

"Thank you, chef," I say, my voice coming out almost in a whisper. She barely nods a response.

"That's a wrap, everyone," says Luis as he stands up from his seat. "Let's get to work."

I work myself up to a standing position even though my legs feel like jelly. I am determined to impress Norah. She isn't exactly the mentor I was hoping for, but maybe she wants me to prove myself first.

Devon was much easier to impress.

21

Several hours later, after a full day of prepping, chopping, blending, and every other food preparation method I have ever learned, I have the first round of desserts ready. Luis has paired me with Alex, a middle-aged man with a bowl haircut and dirty brown eyes. He is fairly quiet and works quickly at any and every request I throw his way.

"So where did you work before Thistle?" I ask him as we set out the dishes side by side.

"A couple of restaurants in New Jersey and New York," he says, not looking up.

"Oh, did you work at Pepper?"

He shakes his head. "No, never."

Well, it appears that Alex isn't much for conversation, which suits me just fine. He's a bit older than me as well, which reminds me how lucky I am to be in this position.

We have about two hours before our first reservation. As Alex and I keep busy, I can't help but wonder why there aren't more people here who worked at Pepper. I mean, it was such a popular restaurant, and surely they had a top-tier kitchen staff. Maybe they just didn't want to move out here to the middle of nowhere.

I look up at the clock. It's four o'clock, the time when Norah and Luis walk around the room, tasting and reviewing every dish prior to dinner.

I have prepared two of Norah's recipes—the macerated strawberries with cream and a yogurt parfait with pistachio crumbles—with precise detail. She may notice tweaks here and there, but I can't imagine she will consider my work a failure in any way. What I am really holding my breath for is how she will like the layered caramel apple tarte I created for tonight.

Alex and I work diligently, plating and preparing the desserts, right up until the moment Norah and Luis are standing in front of our station.

"Chef Sadie, what have you prepared for us today?" says Luis with a Spanish accent. Norah remains quiet, standing just behind his right shoulder.

I walk them through the preparation of Norah's dishes. The two of them listen intently as I gesture toward each dish, revealing nothing of their opinion. Norah leans over one of the desserts and picks up a fork. She carefully lifts a small bite to her mouth.

Alex and I stand with our backs straight, holding our breath. When she nods her approval, we both let out a small exhale. On to the next dish. Norah and Luis both taste this dish, taking their time to ponder over every morsel. Another nod.

Finally, it's time for them to taste my caramel apple tarte. I have artfully plated the dish on one of the long rectangular white plates so that I can add a long line of caramel sauce and a dusting of cinnamon for visual texture. It's practically a Picasso at this point.

"Here we have a caramel apple tarte..." I start to describe the exact dish that I presented in this morning's meeting. Neither Luis nor Norah make eye contact with me as they study the dish. Luis stands with one arm holding one elbow while he rests his chin in his hand. Norah watches with her arms pulled behind her back.

After I finish my description, they both reach for a fresh fork and take turns slicing off a bite to taste. At first, Luis raises his eyebrows, then drops them thoughtfully. Norah's expression is completely stoic.

Luis holds his fork and looks over at Norah. "Hmm? Pretty good, right?"

My heart beats faster.

Norah sets her fork down. "It needs more vanilla in the ice cream. And make sure you wait to add the quenelle of cream until right before the dish is served. None of this sloppy melted cream on the plate."

I swallow. That wasn't so bad. And she didn't say no. She turns and leaves the three of us—Luis, myself, and Alex—standing around the long steel table.

Luis smiles at me. "Relax, Sadie. You did great. She liked it. Trust me, if she didn't like it, it would probably be on the floor by now."

I let out an audible breath now. "So we can serve it on the menu tonight?"

"We'll add it as an option," he says. "Just make the adjustments Norah suggested, and we'll see what happens, okay?"

"Okay," I say, feeling a bit of a flutter in my stomach. "Thank you so much."

He nods and follows Norah to the ovens at the other end

of the kitchen. I turn to Alex. I want to hug him. I want to jump up and down. I want to scream.

Be professional, I tell myself.

"Oh my gosh, she liked it!" I say in a barely contained whisper. Alex gives me a half smile.

"Good work," he says. "I remember when my first dish made it on the menu. What a feeling, right?"

"Incredible," I say. "I hope everyone likes it."

"If Norah and Luis approve, I'm sure they will."

The next couple of hours move by in a blur. At one point, I need to take a bathroom break. While I'm walking down the hall, I bump into Norah.

"Sadie, I'm glad I ran into you," she says.

"Oh?" My shoulders tense.

"The apple tarte is off the menu," she says with a smirk.

"Why?" I feel like someone has punched me in the stomach. Suddenly all the air seems forced out of the room.

"I'm just not sure if it's the right fit for the menu tonight," she says. She begins to walk away. The punch in the gut turns into a fire in my belly. I follow her.

"Wait," I say. As she turns, I falter in my stance. We make eye contact. She arches an eyebrow at me, waiting for me to speak.

"I know about you and Luis," I say.

Now it's her turn to have the wind knocked out of her. She narrows her eyes at me.

"Keep your voice down," she says in a loud whisper. I take a step closer to her until our faces are just six inches apart.

"Put the tarte back on the menu," I say as my hands begin to shake, "or else I'll tell Devon."

I expect her to get angry, maybe even slap me. Instead? *She laughs.*

"Tell Devon? Why, Sadie, be my guest." She takes a step back, turns, and continues down the hall, disappearing into the dining room.

My heart is beating so fast I think it might explode. What does she mean by "be my guest"?

I rush into the bathroom, do my business, and then stare in the mirror. My cheeks are still flushed. *That did not go how I thought it would.*

I take one last deep breath, open the door, and return to my workstation.

"You okay? You're shaking," Alex says.

"Yeah," I say, trying to steady myself. "Just nerves."

Alex and I finish all three dishes up to the point where they're ready to serve. I watch the clock as the first reservations arrive, counting down the minutes until it's time for the desserts to go out.

Minutes stretch on for what feels like hours. A food expo periodically shows up at our station and asks for one of Norah's dishes. Alex and I work quickly to put on the final preparations to make them ready. This happens again. And again. Each time a food runner shows up and asks for Norah's dish, we make haste.

The hours pass, and no one has ordered the apple tarte. Not one. I feel deflated. Maybe it just didn't sound good to anyone? How did they write it up on the menu? A dozen different reasons pop up in my head as to why someone wouldn't order my dish.

"Sadie, how's it going so far?"

I look up to see Devon standing in front of my station, looking subtly hot in a fitted black suit and an unbuttoned collared shirt. The disheveled hair and dark circles under his eyes from this morning are gone.

"Good, I think. It's been steady," I say.

"And your dish, the apple tarte? Did you get any feedback from the servers?"

I shift in my stance. Did Norah even put it on the menu? I honestly don't know. I decide on the simplest answer.

"No one has ordered it yet."

A look passes across his face. "I see," he says. He looks around the room. "Seen Norah anywhere?"

"No, she went out the back twenty minutes ago," I say. I point my chin at the back door.

"Of course she did," he says, almost under his breath. "I'll be back."

I watch as he takes a few long strides to the back door. Once he's gone, a few more of the food runners show up to take orders. It's almost nine thirty at this point, and all the reservations are in for the night. I decide to head to the walk-in freezer to check on the vanilla ice cream I made earlier.

When I open up the freezer, a blast of cold air hits me. I walk inside and look through each row for the tub of ice cream. I can't find it. I know I placed it on the third shelf down on the right. I look again. Nothing.

Where is my ice cream?

I go back to my station and ask Alex if he's pulled it from the freezer. He shakes his head. As I'm scanning the room, a view out the window in front of the dishwasher catches my attention. It's Devon and Norah standing down by the water. Norah is waving her hands, and Devon has his arms crossed. It's clear they are fighting.

We're pretty much done with our shift, so I tell Alex I'm taking a break. I walk to the back door, inching it open. I can hear their voices as the cool night air hits my face. I step outside and into the shadows under the awning by the back door.

"So she's my replacement, huh? You think she can hack it? Make you enough money to pay back those mobsters you're working with?"

"Keep your voice down," Devon says through his teeth, taking a step toward Norah.

"If I go, you know Luis will follow me," she says.

"I wouldn't be so sure about that, Norah."

"Not everything is about money, Devon," she says in a harsh whisper.

Norah begins to pull the strings on her apron, ripping it off her waist.

"I quit," she says.

"You can't quit. You know that," he says.

"Or what? You'll stop caring for her? She'd be better off in a nursing home than stuck in that shitty little cabin."

"You know we can't afford—"

"Well, you'd better figure out how. Because I'm done playing chef," she says. She begins to storm off toward the house behind the main building.

"Wait!" Devon says, chasing after her.

Once the two of them have disappeared into the dark, I take a deep breath. A dozen questions buzz around in my head. *Take care of whom? Do Devon and Norah have a sick child I've never heard of?*

The cabin in the back. The one with the light on at night. There must be someone living there. Someone whom they've kept a secret.

I stare at the empty space where the two of them disappeared. There is so much I don't know about the couple.

Even though I've read every article, watched every YouTube video review on Thistle before I came, there is something I've missed. Something rather important.

I turn and take a step back toward the kitchen door. My foot catches on something, and I stumble forward. I look down. Lying at my feet is a tub of melting ice cream. My handwriting is on the side. A sick feeling settles in my stomach. Heat rises up to my cheeks. Someone intentionally sabotaged my ice cream.

The question is, *why?*

22

Of course, I barely sleep that night. I walk to the window a couple of times to look at the cabin at the back of the property, but there are no lights on. Then I start to question myself. Maybe I didn't see a light on over there. The hours at Thistle have been long, and I practically collapse into my bed each night, only to wake up a few hours later.

I've heard that sleep deprivation can drive you insane, or cause hallucinations at the very least. Is my mind playing tricks on me?

I stare into the darkness. Norah is the other reason I can't sleep. I showed my hand tonight by threatening to reveal her affair. And her reaction? She laughed. So Devon must know about her and Luis. They must have some type of open marriage.

And why did she allow me to prepare the apple tarte if she was just going to take it off the menu? She could have just said she didn't like it to my face. I don't know Norah well, but from what I've seen, she doesn't seem to have a problem voicing her opinion.

Was it jealousy? Surely she isn't jealous of my cooking. Compared to her, I am nothing. A complete newbie in her world. Just the fact that she let me cook her recipes was an honor. I'm younger than her by ten years, but I'm pretty frumpy relative to her refined good looks.

So why does she hate me so much?

Regardless of what's in that cabin, there is definitely something strange going on with the Winthrops. Not just the affair between Norah and Luis. Something they are trying to hide.

I crawl into bed and toss and turn for the rest of the night.

WHEN I WALK into the kitchen for my next shift, I've got a pounding headache. Business continues as usual. After a couple of hours of prep, it's time for the morning meeting in the dining room. The kitchen staff sits down at the long dining table to present recipes, but two people are noticeably absent.

Norah and Luis.

Devon walks in and stands at the head of the table.

"Good morning, everyone," he says, pulling his shoulders back to their full height. "Norah and Luis left this morning for a meeting in New York. They won't be back for the shift this evening."

There are a couple of murmurs in the room. Devon clears his throat.

"One of the things I am most proud of at Thistle is how

our kitchen operates like a well-oiled machine. So tonight is an opportunity for each of you to step up and show me your best work."

So they left. Norah and Luis. They left *together.*

I wrinkle my forehead. Is Devon lying? Did they really leave on a work trip, or did Norah actually quit? I look around the room and realize I am the only one who must be worried. Probably because I am the only one who heard them arguing last night.

"Sadie, what do you have for us today?" Devon's voice breaks up my thoughts.

"I, um, was thinking of making Norah's recipe for poached peaches with vanilla crisp. We received a fresh bushel of peaches this morning."

Devon nods. "And do you have anything of your own to share?"

"No," I say, my voice barely a whisper in the large room. I can feel the staff staring at me.

He frowns. "Why don't you try to come up with something, and I'll check in with you in an hour."

My shoulders slump. I feel I have disappointed Devon. The truth is, I do have an idea for a dish, but what's the point? The incident with Norah has shaken my confidence.

"Okay," I say.

"Alright, that's a wrap," Devon says as he stands. "I will be doing the tasting today, so I'll see you all in a few hours."

Devon leaves the room and heads to the side exit. I follow the line of kitchen staff back toward the kitchen. To my surprise, the mood in the room is of excitement. They are chattering and laughing. It's almost if they're excited that Norah is gone. I guess I can't blame them; it's not like she's the easiest chef to work for. As I reach the door to the kitchen, I see Alex waiting for me.

"Hey, Sadie," he says. "What do you think is going on?"

My heart beats wildly. "Going on?"

"Yeah, I mean, come on. Why would Norah and Luis leave on a work trip right before our Saturday night shift? That doesn't make any sense."

I keep my expression neutral. "She must really trust us," I say. Even though I know it's not true. There is definitely something strange going on.

But I'm not about to share what I know. Not yet.

Alex snorts. "Listen, I've been around this business long enough to have seen a few things. And there is definitely something weird going on," he says. "And I've heard a few of them whispering about you getting in Devon's car and him stopping by your cabin. I would steer clear if I were you."

A little heat creeps up my cheeks. "He's just my boss," I say.

"Right," Alex says as we arrive at our workstation. "I'll start working on the poached peaches."

I've made the right decision to keep quiet, I know it. But what I don't know is what is really going on at Thistle. And it's time for me to find out.

23

Dinner that night goes rather smoothly, even without Norah and Luis there. Devon was right about the well-oiled machine. I just wonder how long the machine can last without Norah.

It's only my second night as Charlie's replacement, but I feel like I've hit my rhythm. I keep it professional with Alex, even though I'm a little irked that he basically accused me of sleeping with the boss. The two of us work side by side, feeling and anticipating each other's moves as we prepare each dish carefully for the night.

My thoughts for the rest of the shift are strictly of slicing, baking, preparing, and composition. But not far from those thoughts are all the strange things that keep happening around me at Thistle. Every restaurant has its secrets, but this isn't what I expected when I started working here.

It's certainly not what I dreamed of.

Even though I only have one goal, to stay here for the résumé boost and make connections, I still can't help but wonder what's going on.

It's past ten o'clock, and the energy of the kitchen staff has dropped. I look around and see the chefs starting to clean up their stations and wrap up for the night.

"That's the last reservation, team," Devon says from the center of the room. I've been extremely impressed with how Devon stepped in to run the kitchen tonight. He rolled up his sleeves and worked with the staff, building them up, stepping in when needed. He may not have Norah's chef skills, but he's much better at working with a team than she is.

After he makes the announcement and leaves, Alex and I get to work cleaning. As I'm stacking dishes up at the washing station, Ingrid approaches me.

"Sadie," she says. My heart drops. Surely it's not the Grissom family again. "Devon would like to see you in his office."

"Oh, okay," I say. I make eye contact with Alex. He raises his eyebrows at me. I want to tell him that just because the boss wants to talk to me, it doesn't mean we're sleeping together. Alex speaks up before I can say anything.

"Go," he says. "I can finish up."

"Thanks." I can't shake the comment he made earlier. That he heard whispers of Devon coming to my cabin. The same whispers I heard from the waitstaff. I shake my head. Let them talk; I haven't done anything.

I pull off my apron and drop it in the laundry bin as I walk down the hall. I'm still warm from working in the kitchen, so when the cool night air hits my skin, it feels refreshing. But after a few seconds, I'm rubbing my arms. I wish I had grabbed my sweater.

I knock twice on the door when I reach the milk house.

"Come in," says Devon from inside.

I nudge the door open and step inside. I can't help but look up as I walk into the room; you can actually see the stars through the large skylights overhead.

"Pretty cool, isn't it? I can see the Little Dipper from my desk," he says.

"Yes, really cool," I manage. I return my gaze to Devon. His jacket is slung over the back of his chair, and his shirt is unbuttoned down to his chest. There's a bottle of open bourbon on the table, and a couple of glasses.

"Ingrid said you wanted to see me?"

"Yes, have a seat," he says. "Drink?"

"No, I'm good," I say.

"Come on, this is Pappy's 12 year. Legendary stuff," he says.

I push my mouth to one side. Nothing sounds better than a stiff drink right now. I'm just not sure I trust myself drinking around my boss. But as Devon looks at me, I realize I can't say no either.

"Okay, sure," I say. He pours me a glass, neat. I'm not much of a bourbon drinker, but we did a few tastings when I was working at Château Bernard, and it's not so bad.

Devon places the glass in front of me and raises his. "Cheers," he says. "To a successful night."

"Cheers," I say.

I take a sip of the bourbon, which burns my throat, but in a good way. Devon downs his drink in one gulp, then pours himself another. I can't help but think of Alex right now, judging me as he cleans our station.

"So what did you want to see me about?" I ask. He takes another swig of his bourbon and sets it down on the desk.

"Can you keep a secret?"

I almost laugh despite myself. *He has no idea.*

"Of course," I say.

"Norah and Luis are not on a work trip," he says. "They left."

I knew it!

"Left, as in for good?"

"Yes." He nods, finishes his drink, and pours himself another. I grip my glass in my hand, barely taking a sip. "With my blessing."

I feel my jaw drop to the floor. *So he knows about the affair.* I try to come up with something to say, but instead take a drink.

"But aren't you married?"

He shrugs. "For now. Norah and I have been together for a long time. And our marriage has become more of a business relationship than a marriage. After a while, we just fell out of love with each other. But we still wanted the same things. We still had the same dream."

He leans back in his leather armchair, which creaks under the pressure of his body. "But things have changed. Norah wants to be with Luis. She's burnt out on the restaurant industry. And so we've decided to get a divorce."

My brain spins. This is so much more information than I expected.

"Why are you telling me this?"

"Because I think you're ready to take things to the next level."

"Next level?"

Devon sighs and shifts in his seat. He looks me directly in the eyes. "How would you like to prepare a winter menu for Thistle? Five courses. Just like the menu you described to me on the way back from the oyster farm."

My heart flutters. He's talking about the "what-if" menu. The one I've been working on since I got here.

"I will supply the main ingredient list," he continues, "and you can make recommendations on what else you might need. If I like what I see, we can do a test run next weekend."

I set my glass down on the table. He wants me to design a menu for Thistle? I want to scream *yes!* But I'm too stunned to say anything.

"Why me?"

"As I have told you before, Sadie, you have a talent. That menu you came up with in the van? That was perfect, the type of creativity I haven't seen in years. Not to mention the press will eat you up. You know you're very attractive, right?"

I blush.

"Norah is pretty, but she's not relatable. It was the food that brought people. But you have both the talent and the personality."

I rub the tops of my legs, trying to process his offer.

"Are you sure the kitchen staff will be okay with this? I mean, Norah had this great reputation...isn't that why they're all here?"

Devon shakes his head. "Do you remember the other night when we had rumors of a Michelin inspector at the restaurant?"

I nod.

"Well, they did come. But we didn't get the star."

"Why?"

"Normally, you never find out why. But I know some people." He spins the glass in his hands and then leans forward. "And it turns out the reason we didn't get the star is because of Norah. Her recipes have become repetitive and stale. I need a new chef with new ideas. A chef like you, Sadie."

Devon's blue eyes bore into mine. He's probably wondering why I haven't said yes yet. I mean, this is the opportunity I've been dreaming of my whole career. It's beyond anything I could have dreamed when Norah hired me.

But something in my gut, something is making me hesitate, even if it's just for a split second.

"So what do you think? Need a few days to think it over?"

I reach for the glass on the table and take the final sip. "No," I say, placing it back. "I'll do it."

"Great," he says, getting up from his seat. "I'll have the list over to you in the morning."

I stand as well, not sure what to do next. I'm still in shock from his offer. He walks to the door and opens it for me. I walk a few steps to follow him, looking around the room for what feels like the first time.

There are large wooden bookshelves on both walls. There are awards, pictures of a few restaurants, and a row of law books. I read somewhere that Devon was a lawyer for a few years before teaming up with Norah to start their restaurant.

A small framed photograph catches my attention. I take a step toward it on my way to the door. I pause long enough to see younger versions of Devon and Norah, plus another woman who looks just like her. They're practically twins.

"Does Norah have a sister?"

"Oh, well, yes. She's a few years older. Lives in Seattle with her family," he says with a dismissive wave of his hands.

"Oh," I say, continuing toward the door. There's something about Norah's sister that looks familiar. I'm not sure why. I keep walking toward the door.

As I pass Devon in the doorway, I pause for a moment and look at him. A mix of bourbon and sandalwood is emanating from his body. For a moment, I lose myself. He's so close.

"Thank you," I say, standing just a few inches from him, "for giving me this opportunity."

We lock eyes for a moment, and I forget that he's married. Well, separated, I guess. But he's still my boss.

Then to my surprise, Devon leans down and kisses me on the cheek. I feel a jolt of pleasure course through my body.

"You're welcome, Sadie," he whispers, so close to my face it tickles my cheek. "Good night."

I hurry past him and out the door. I'm afraid if I stand there a second longer, we might cross the line between professional and personal. The bourbon has warmed me to my core, but I'm afraid to let my guard down.

The starry sky looms above me as I practically skip back to my cabin. A full five-course menu for Thistle. Designed by me. I couldn't have dreamed up a better offer. To create a menu for a famous restaurant.

I probably won't sleep for the next three nights, putting together the perfect menu. I know I don't deserve this opportunity, but I'm going to give it everything I have regardless. For a bittersweet moment, I wish I could call my dad and share the news. He would be so proud of me.

That night, I'm so preoccupied with thoughts of my new menu that I don't even waste my time thinking about the light coming from the cabin in the back of the property.

24

Normally the first part of the week is for food prep. But Devon has closed the kitchen Monday and Tuesday this week, giving all the staff a few extra days off. The farm is practically empty except for a few food vendors who have come to drop off goods or meet with Devon. I've spent the last two days working in the kitchen.

Devon loaned me a company laptop to work with, which is now sitting in front of me on a large stainless-steel workstation. I've been working on the menu for the whole restaurant, poring over websites for ideas, riffling through my cookbooks and old notes. I have a dozen sketches of food, ingredients, and recipes scattered around the table. The kitchen is empty, which is unusual. The sun set at least an hour ago—I think it did, anyway; I've lost track of time. One lamp in the kitchen hangs over the table, shedding light on my work.

Devon has given me carte blanche, and to be honest, it's a little bit intimidating.

I try to stick to simple ingredients with a few twists.

We're expecting a large delivery of oysters this week, and I had an idea to do an oysters Rockefeller with bacon, shallots, arugula, white Stilton cheese, and then garnish it with an edible flower called nasturtium. I bite the tip of my finger. I'm hoping the flower is enough to elevate the dish, but I'm not certain.

Part of me wishes I could get a little feedback from Norah right now. But then, judging by how she ditched my freshly made ice cream on the porch, she'd probably burn down the whole idea.

"Nasturtium and oysters, huh? I like it," I hear a voice say behind me. Devon must have come in the back door of the kitchen, because I didn't hear him come in. I feel a little heat rise in my cheeks.

"Thanks," I say. "I hope it's good enough."

Devon pulls up a stool and sits next to me. "I'm sure it will be fabulous. The team will be here to help you as well." He looks over my notes. "It looks like you've made a lot of progress already."

I nod. "I have a good first draft."

I'm trying to sound confident, but in truth, this could go either way. He may hate what I've put together, or love it.

"Well, I think it's time for a break," he says. "Come on, follow me."

Devon starts walking toward the dining room. I tuck a few strands of hair behind my ears and follow him. I'm sure I look like a mess. We walk for a few moments in silence, but when he opens the swinging door to the dining room, I catch my breath.

Placed on a small white-clothed table is a bottle of wine and two plates of food. As I get closer, I spot a salad topped with nuts and some kind of crumbled cheese, toasted garlic bread, and a plate of lasagna.

Devon pulls out the chair for me. I feel a little silly, sitting down in the quiet dining room with my black tee shirt and work pants. Devon takes a seat across from me. He reaches over and pours each of us a glass of red wine. There are a couple of small candles lit between us, and Devon has some music playing in the background.

"Did you make this?"

"Yes," he says with a smile. He pours me nearly a full glass of wine. I notice he's showered and shaved. I feel slightly underdressed. I'm sure I could use a splash of lip gloss and a brush for my hair.

"I'm no chef, but my mother used to make me this lasagna when I was a kid. It was my favorite."

I'm touched that he cooked for me. I take a few sips of wine, which hits my empty stomach and warms my belly, then take a bite of the lasagna.

"Oh wow, this is really good," I say. And I mean it. It's really good lasagna. Devon smiles as he chews a few bites of his own, then swallows.

"That's a nice compliment coming from you, chef," he says with a wink.

I shake my head. "I still can't believe it."

"You'll get used to the title, trust me. This is what you're meant for," he says.

"It's better than working in a diner, that's for sure," I say. Devon laughs. As the two of us eat, we swap stories of our worst jobs. Me, working at Mike's Diner. Devon had a whole string of horrible jobs, like working in a marina shucking oysters, and cleaning stalls at a horse farm. I'm impressed, to be honest. Even though he must have grown up wealthy, his parents still made him work.

"Oh, I love this song," he says as he gets up from the table. "Dance with me?"

I feel a little flutter in my stomach. I know what it means when a guy asks you to dance in a room alone. And as I look at the earnest look on Devon's face as he holds his hand out to me, I know what will happen if I accept.

The truth is that I've been attracted to Devon since the day I met him. But now we're going to be working together. *Closely.* Traditional wisdom says mixing business with pleasure is never a good idea.

But then, I've never been good at making wise decisions.

"Yes," I say, reaching out to accept his hand. We spend a few minutes dancing in the dining room of Thistle, our bodies intertwined.

And before I know it, Devon Winthrop and I are kissing.

25

I wake up Wednesday morning alone in my bed. I stare at the ceiling, the rough-hewn beams staring back at me. The curtains are slightly split, with just a touch of light creating a soft glow in the room. I pull the sheets up to my neck, covering my naked body.

I wasn't alone the whole evening. Devon came home with me last night. The dance in the dining room led to kissing, which led to the two of us stumbling back to the cabin together.

I knew from the first kiss that the sex was going to be good. But Devon surprised me. It was even better than I imagined. Then again, it had been a while for me. I hadn't slept with anyone since Peter.

I reach over and rub the sheets where he was lying last night. The spot is cold, which means he probably left in the middle of the night. I'm not sure how I feel about this. I'm sure he doesn't want the staff to see him doing the walk of shame from my cabin in the morning. Either way, it was worth it.

I reach over to the nightstand and grab my phone. It's almost eight a.m., which means it's time for me to head to the kitchen and prepare for the day. I get dressed and make my way to the bathroom, which is now in complete working order. As I do, something catches my attention.

Hanging on the back of the dining room chair is a white chef's coat. I walk toward it. The right side has *Thistle* embroidered on it. Underneath is my name: *Chef Sadie Jackson*.

I run my fingers over the embroidery. *It's really happening.*

A few minutes later I'm walking through the back door of the kitchen. Most of the staff are already there, chopping, basting, and baking. Business as usual. I practically run to my workstation, where all of my recipes are still spread out.

I start organizing the menu when Ingrid suddenly appears by my side, towering over me. She has her signature sharp bun pulling back her temples. I can smell the faint hint of lavender on her skin.

"Good morning, Sadie." She looks at me with her piercing eyes. "Devon has instructed me to assist you today. He says you'll be working on a new test menu that we'll be sampling tonight."

"Where is Devon?"

Ingrid clears her throat. "He was called away on some business."

My shoulders slump. After last night, I assumed he would be here with me today. Or that he would at least say goodbye before he left my bed this morning.

"Oh," I reply. I pull together my recipe notes and hold them up in front of her. "Here's the menu. I'm excited to share it with the staff."

Ingrid looks over my shoulder, scanning my notes and

sketches. I hold my breath, expecting her to respond in some way.

"Hmm." Then she takes a breath. "I'll have everyone assemble in the dining room when they arrive. That way you can instruct them on the menu." She turns and leaves the room, her kitten heels clicking against the tile as she leaves.

Ingrid's reception of my work was a bit cold, but I don't expect everyone to love the fact that I'm the new chef here. I hope they give me a chance. An hour later, the kitchen staff are assembled in the dining room. I take my place at the head of the table. Ingrid has made copies of all the recipes that I put together for the five-course menu.

I scan the room. The staff are scanning my menu. Some of them look concerned, whispering to each other. Others are already making notes on the papers they've been given.

Ingrid clears her throat.

"Good morning, everyone. Sadie has put together a new menu for us. She will be in charge of the kitchen at Thistle moving forward."

There are more murmurs and even a few gasps that float around the room.

I swallow. This might be more difficult than Devon thinks it's going to be. I'm young. I'm new. And I'm sure the staff is less than enthusiastic about me being their new boss.

Ingrid clears her throat. "I know that many of you may be skeptical about trying out a new menu."

Or a new chef, I think.

"Devon couldn't be with us today, but he has prepared a statement he would like me to read to all of you."

Ingrid pulls out a sheet of paper, straightens her back, and begins to read.

"I know many of you are apprehensive about a new chef,

but I assure you that Sadie is talented, creative, and a rising star in our industry. She has put together a five-course menu that I believe each of you can successfully execute. In order to help with the transition, I will be giving you each a bonus of five hundred dollars for the success of this new menu after the first weekend of service. I hope this shows you my appreciation as we transition to a new future here at Thistle."

I watch as the staff exchange looks around the table. *So that's how he's going to convince them.* Of course, he knows that the staff are going to be skeptical of me, and incentivizing them with a bonus will motivate them to do a great job. It's actually a brilliant idea, and I can't help but beam with pride at the intelligence of my new...

My new boyfriend?

"At this point I will leave it to Sadie to talk you through some of the recipes," says Ingrid.

I stand up from my seat and take a deep breath. The notes in my hand are rattling like a leaf.

"Good morning, everyone. I want to thank you in advance for taking a chance on this menu," I say. My voice shakes. A dozen pairs of eyes narrow on me. I clear my throat. "In this room, there are more years of combined experience than I have been alive."

A ripple of chuckles floats around the table.

"So I'm hoping that you will not only recreate the menu I've designed, but also give me your feedback on how we can make it better. I'm excited to learn something from each of you."

The tone in the room shifts. My words seem to put everyone at ease. Or at the very least, they are willing to give me a chance.

I start working my way through the menu. As each chef provides feedback on their dish, I feel my shoulders relax.

I *might* actually be able to pull this off.

A FEW HOURS LATER, the staff and I have assembled the first round of the new menu. The five-course menu includes Russian oscietra caviar, Maine oysters, a lobster and squash bisque, Wagyu filet mignon, and for dessert a chocolate mousse served with rose petals. I pull out all the stops, hoping to make a great first impression.

I feel a drumming in my chest as we put on the final touches. This is everything I've been working for since I left prison. The reason I've lugged around all of the frayed recipe books in my car for the last couple of years. The time I spent at CIA. The way I hustled at Château Bernard. All of that work has finally led me to this moment.

I walk into the dining room. I'm relieved to see Devon is back. He's sitting across the table from Ingrid at a table set for two. There's a white tablecloth, candlelight, and even flowers. Each of them has a flight of wineglasses sitting in front of them for the wine pairing I put together. I will be walking through each item of the menu as I serve them.

When I see Devon, I feel a small tingle of excitement. Last night was amazing. He looks up, and our eyes meet. He gives me a knowing smile.

For a moment, I'm distracted by this. Our time between the sheets last night flashes through my mind. I'm sure he wants us to be discreet about our relationship, and I have no problem with that. Although, the way the staff have been treating me over the last couple of weeks, I'm pretty sure they'll figure it out soon enough.

The first course, oscietra caviar with lemon gelée, arrives at the table. I feel my heart about to beat out of my chest. I stand in front of the table in my chef's coat and walk them through the first menu item.

"The first item on our menu is a locally sourced..." I begin. Over the next hour I present each item in the menu, in detail. I study the facial expressions of Devon and Ingrid with each bite of food.

True to form, Ingrid reveals nothing of her opinion. Devon, on the other hand, seems impressed. He frequently compliments me on the food and even makes a few small suggestions.

At the end of the meal as they're taking the last few bites of mousse, Devon places his spoon on the table and leans back. He looks up at me with a wide smile.

"Chef, that was fantastic," he says. My chest swells. I nod my thanks.

"Nice work, chef," says Ingrid. Her approval feels like a special victory, given she doesn't dole out a lot of compliments.

The busser comes out and clears the table. I stand back. Devon and Ingrid lean together and speak quietly. Once the table is clear, Ingrid stands up.

"Good luck," she says.

"Thanks," I say as she leaves the room. Devon and I are alone in the dining room. He stands up and walks over to me, placing his hands on my shoulders.

"Congratulations," he says. Then he leans close to my ear and whispers, "How about we celebrate later tonight at the cabin?"

I feel a tingle of excitement that starts in my toes and ends in my fingers.

"Sounds good to me," I say. He touches my hand for a brief moment, then walks out the side exit toward his office. I practically levitate my way back to the kitchen. I breathe in deep and let the air out of my lungs.

The menu is a success. I can tell they were impressed. Even better? I have a celebration to look forward to later.

26

A few hours later, I'm lying naked in my bed with Devon's arms wrapped around me. The bedcovers are hanging off the bed, our clothes scattered around the room. I think about what he just did to me and shiver with pleasure. Norah is crazy for letting this man get away.

Devon must be having the same thoughts, because he leans over to me and brushes the hair out of my face.

"You're amazing, Sadie."

"So are you," I say, touching his hand.

I lean over and start kissing him again, but before things can get too heated, he pulls away. He props himself up on the bed and looks at me.

"I have some work to finish up in the office tonight. I've reached out to my PR team to share the news that we have a new chef at Thistle." He presses his thumb against my chin. "I can't wait for everyone to try your menu."

I cock my head to one side. Of course I wish he were staying the night. But I understand.

"Are you sure you don't want to stay?" I puff out my bottom lip.

"I wish I could," he says. He reaches over and kisses me again. For a moment, things get heated. And I think he's going to stay. But then he pulls away and slides out the side of the bed. I watch him get dressed, lying in bed with a sheet only covering the bottom half of my body.

"You make it hard to leave," he says, putting on his last shoe. "Get some rest. You have a big day tomorrow."

"Goodbye," I say as he walks out the door. After staring at the ceiling for a few minutes, I get up to take a shower. The steam wraps around me, relaxing every muscle in my body. By the time I lie back down in bed, I'm so relaxed that I fall asleep after a few minutes.

A FAINT NOISE wakes me up in the middle of the night. Probably a raccoon trying to get into one of the dumpsters out back. I realize I'm still wearing my shower robe.

I fumble around in the darkness for the light switch, flip it on and walk over to the small chest of drawers to find some flannel pants. As I do, I hear the sound again.

Walking over to the window, I pull back the curtain and peer into the dark. My heartbeat picks up. I pull on a pair of jeans instead with a tee shirt and run to the window. I could have sworn I heard something. But when I look out into the inky darkness, I don't see or hear anything.

At some point I have to get this insomnia under control.

I walk past the window again. This time, I see a light. The same light that I've seen half a dozen times, coming from the cabin across the lake.

With everything going on with my new position here at Thistle, I had pushed it to the back of my mind. It seems that I've learned most of the secrets of Thistle, but is there something else I don't know about?

At that point, my curiosity gets the best of me. It's time for me to find out what's happening back there once and for all.

I find a sweater hanging off one of the small chairs in the room and pull it on. Stepping into the boots sitting by the door, I exit quietly into the night.

It only takes me about ten minutes to close the distance from my cabin around the lake to the cabin on the back of the property. It's strangely quiet this time of night. I can hear the sound of dead leaves crunching under my feet, only broken periodically by an owl in the distance.

I pull the sleeves of my sweater over my hands. It's colder than I thought it would be. As I get closer to the cabin, I start to second-guess myself. What would Devon think if he found me walking around the property in the middle of the night?

Well, I know that Devon doesn't sleep here. He stays at the large farmhouse on the other end of the property closest to the restaurant. I know it's not Luis, and it's definitely not Norah.

I'm about ten feet away now. The light is on in the window, but the curtains are closed. I can only see a few shadows inside. My palms begin to sweat. I try to peer through the curtains, but I can't make out anything in the room except for the dark shadows. I walk up to the front door.

Again, I feel a little ridiculous out here, but I'm so close now I can't stop.

I'm standing in front of the door. A cold chill passes up my spine. My hand pauses in the air, suspended over the doorknob.

Something in my gut tells me this is a very bad idea. I take a deep breath. It's time to find out what is going on in this cabin. With a deep breath, I knock and, hearing no response, cautiously open the door and walk inside.

The layout of the cabin is almost identical to mine. There's a kitchen with a coffee machine on the left side of the room, a dining table near the front. But instead of a sofa in the center of the room, there's a large blue recliner.

A woman is sitting there, staring into space.

The woman in the chair isn't moving. But I know she's seen me because she's staring right at me. I wave my hands in front of her.

"Hello?" I say. "I'm Sadie."

She doesn't move. She doesn't even blink. I wave again. Nothing.

I step closer and look at her. The woman has shoulder-length dark brown hair and pale green eyes.

And that's when I feel my heart explode. It's as if someone has taken a shard of glass and stabbed me in the heart. I stand there for a few seconds, letting recognition of the person in front of me sink in.

Because the person sitting in the recliner is Norah Winthrop.

In that moment, I realize I've made a very big mistake.

PART II

NAOMI

27

"This is it. We're free," Luis says as he reaches over the table and squeezes my hand. I quickly look over my shoulder. *Free.*

I hope he's right.

We're sitting outside at a café in New York. With the hustle of the city, we are pretty much invisible to everyone around us. Anonymity is easy to find when you're in a sea of millions. That's probably why so many people are intimidated by the city. But being unseen has never felt so welcome.

A small sense of peace begins to unfold inside me. Part of it is because we've left Devon behind. *Finally.*

The other reason? I can actually see a future ahead of us. A future that doesn't involve a restaurant teetering on the brink of bankruptcy and a group of debt collectors on our heels. A future free of the lie I've been telling everyone over the last couple of years.

My name is not Norah, it's Naomi.

And Norah Winthrop is my sister.

Three Years Earlier

"CHEERS TO US," I repeat as the three of us—Devon, Norah, and myself—clink glasses. We're sitting around a small steel workstation in the back of our newly minted restaurant, Pepper.

"I can't believe we did it," Norah says. "We pulled it off."

"What was it the paper said?" Devon asks. He pulls the magazine in front of him and reads the article out loud. "The future hit restaurant of New York has just landed on West Fifteenth Street. Get a reservation before the six-month wait-list arrives."

We all laugh as he waves the magazine over our heads. It has been six months since we started dreaming up the restaurant. And by some miracle, the three of us have pulled it off.

Devon and Norah have been dating for about a year. I always thought Devon was handsome, with his thick auburn hair, blue eyes, and movie-star smile. Who wouldn't find him attractive?

And Norah? She's slender, with those big green eyes and dark hair. I've heard others describe her as striking.

Two gorgeous, talented, and motivated Manhattanites in their thirties. I knew from day one that those two would end up together. And now? They run a successful business together.

Along with me, of course.

"Here's to my incredibly smart boyfriend, who by some miracle got us a lease on this fantastic space," says Norah. Devon gives a satisfied smile.

It really does feel like a miracle. He found us a terrific piece of real estate in Manhattan. It has about 3,300 square feet with a private mezzanine. I'm still not sure how he was able to afford it. With his Italian leather loafers and cashmere sweaters, he reeks of old money, but I've never gotten a clear picture of where the money comes from.

Whatever the source, we had an eclectic space to work with that had exposed brick walls and a large fireplace in the center of the room. My sister practically cried when she saw it for the first time.

"And to my sister, Naomi, for keeping everything running smoothly," she says.

"Stop it; you're making me blush!" I reach over and give her a playful punch on the shoulder. We all laugh. "But seriously, I know I didn't contribute the money that Devon did."

I hold my glass out to him. His eyes shift sideways even as he smiles, and that familiar suspicion squeezes my stomach.

It's old family money, I tell myself. And he's a lawyer. Lawyers make money.

So I go on.

"And my sister, of course, who's the greatest chef the world has ever seen." I hold my glass up to her. She rolls her eyes in a good-natured way.

I point to myself with the glass as I say, "But I'm just lucky to be here with you both. I have job-hopped for the last decade, and I finally feel like I'm doing something right. So thank you. And here's to Pepper."

We clink our glasses together. While Norah and Devon met building their careers, I've always been a bit of a free spirit. I've worked in restaurants, in traveling carnivals, and I even had a stint at an auto body shop. But working with my sister at Pepper the last three months is the most at home I've ever felt.

Two and a Half Years Ago

"ARE you sure you want to do this?" I ask Norah as we stand in the back pantry. I followed her here, knowing we would have a chance to speak alone, without prying ears listening in.

"Do what?" she asks, rummaging through a few sacks of flour.

"Marry Devon," I say in a loud whisper. She stops looking through the flour and stares at me. The love between Norah and Devon seems to have gone sour. The fighting has escalated to a physical level. At first I noticed a few bruises on her arm. Then a bruise on her shoulder. But the worst was two weeks ago, she had a black eye. She tried to cover it up with makeup, but I know he hit her.

No matter how many times I bring it up, she refuses to admit he's hurting her. I know Norah. Once she gets something in her head, it's impossible to change her mind.

"Of course, why would you ask me that?"

"I'm your sister." I give her a knowing look. "And you two don't seem to be getting along."

Norah swipes her bangs with the backs of her hands. The long hours at the restaurant have begun to take a toll on her. She looks thin, a bit gaunt. I wonder if she's actually eating any of the food she cooks.

"Oh, Naomi, come on. All couples fight," she says.

"Not like that," I say, pointing to the bruise on her arm. She pulls her sleeve down.

"It's not what you think," she says. "Besides, you've never even been in a serious relationship before. Devon and I are building a big future. With the restaurant. We may even open a second location. It's a lot of pressure."

I roll my eyes. With Norah, it's all about the restaurant. She's *obsessed.* I'm worried it's clouding her judgment.

"Are you sure you can trust him?"

"What do you mean, Naomi?" She continues rummaging around in the stainless-steel rack of supplies.

"Norah, you saw those men leave his office last night. You can't tell me—"

"Tell you what? He handles all of our accounts. Of course he meets with a lot of people."

"At ten o'clock at night? In a room he soundproofed?"

"Okay," Norah says, spinning on me and folding her arms on her chest. "Show me proof. If you're so sure he's up to something, what is it? We order supplies, we pay for them, and we receive them. What is he doing wrong?"

I clench my fists. How can she not see it? Devon is bad news. He's crooked. I just know it. But I'm not sure how to tell Norah all this. I mean, she loves him. And seems determined to marry him. I sigh.

"Never mind," I say. "Listen, I know this is a bad time, but there's something I have been meaning to tell you."

"Found it!" Norah says, pulling out a sack of self-rising flour. "What is it?"

Seeing her standing there with a sack of flour in her hands and a smudge on her face, I hesitate to say what I'm about to tell her.

But here goes. "I'm leaving."

Norah drops the sack, and a puff of flour hangs in the air between us. "What?! You can't!"

"Oh, come on, Norah. You guys don't need me here. There are probably a hundred other people in the city who are more qualified and better at my job."

Norah looks like she's going to argue with me. But then she slumps her shoulders. "Why do you want to leave?"

"It's just not the place for me. I want to see more of the world. Here I just feel like a third wheel."

"You know you're part owner of Pepper, right?"

"Yes, but only you and Devon know that. Can't you just buy me out?"

Norah bites her lip. "Maybe at some point. Right now? With the rent increasing and the higher price of food...not to mention the cost of employees, benefit—"

I hold up my hand to stop her. "It's okay. I get it. Listen, I'll be back in a year. We can talk about it then."

"Where are you going?"

"I found a waitressing gig on a private yacht. Sailing around the Caribbean and South America."

Norah smiles. "That sounds like you."

"Right?" I reach over and hug her. "I am going to miss you though, little sis."

"I'll miss you too," she says. We hold each other for a moment, which is interrupted by one of the kitchen staff screaming for more flour.

"But you'll stay for the wedding?"

I shift my feet. "Actually, the boat leaves Tuesday."

Norah frowns at me. Another scream from the kitchen.

"I have to go," she says as she walks toward the door. "We will talk about this later!"

Norah gives me one last look before disappearing into the kitchen.

28

ONE AND A HALF YEARS AGO

When I step off the boat and onto land for the first time in months, it's the humidity that hits me first. The Florida humidity. It's like walking into a wall of steam.

I'm happy to be back on land though. The last year of sailing has been incredible, but I'm the first to admit I like a bit more room. I stretch my fingers, which are stiff from tying knots and scrubbing decks. It feels so good to be in an open space, I want to run laps up and down the boardwalk.

Being a shipmate has had its benefits though, one of which was meeting Luis.

"Are you ready to go?" he asks as he lugs my bags down the dock.

"Yes, let's go reconnect with the world," I say as he leans in to kiss me.

Luis was the private chef for the couple who rented the yacht. I've worked enough restaurants to know that Luis is extremely talented, organized, and resourceful. I actually learned a lot from him.

More importantly, he makes me tingle all over when he touches my body. And he's hot. So naturally he's become my boyfriend. And since neither of us had anywhere to run outside of the twenty-five-thousand-square-foot yacht we were on, our relationship blossomed.

Luis and I are headed to the local electronics store in Fort Lauderdale to have my cell phone service reinstated. To save money and, really, for my own sanity, I decided to have my service shut off while we were at sea. Not that I have many close friends except for my sister.

About an hour later, my phone is powered on and set to receive messages. I stand outside in the parking lot, watching them pop up, one after another.

There are a few from my sister, but mostly fairly recent missed calls and texts from Devon. Which is strange. Why does Devon need to speak with me so badly? I frown at my phone.

Something's off.

First, I dial Norah's phone. It goes straight to voicemail. It's the middle of the day, so she's probably working. Then I dial Devon's number. After a few rings, he picks up.

"Devon, it's Naomi," I say.

"Naomi, are you back?" The desperation in his voice makes me sweat.

"Yes, I'm here in Florida. Is everything okay?"

"No, there's been an accident. I need you to come to New York right away."

The sick feeling in my stomach gets stronger. "Is Norah okay?"

There's a pause. "She's stable. We're at the hospital now. It's better we talk in person. I'm sending our location to your phone."

I see a location pop up on my phone. "Okay, I got it."

"Great. See you soon." And he hangs up.

Luis walks out of the store. When he sees the look on my face, his dark brows knit together in concern.

"Naomi, is everything okay?"

"No," I say, slightly stunned. "We need to go to New York, now."

A HALF A DAY LATER, Luis drives me up to a small office building on the outskirts of the city. Devon said Norah was in an accident and that she was in the hospital. But this is a different kind of hospital than I'm used to seeing. There are no large signs out front. You wouldn't know it was a hospital unless someone told you. Devon is waiting for us in the parking lot.

"Naomi, I'm so glad you're here." He walks up and gives me a long hug. I pull back. He looks haggard, his usually carefully clipped hair hanging over his ears.

"What's going on?" There are about a million alarm bells going off in my head. It's time to get some answers.

"There was a fire at Pepper," he says. "It burned the entire place down. Norah was burned badly."

He looks away from me as he speaks. There's pain in his eyes. I'm too stunned to speak. I want to throw up.

"I didn't want anyone to find out because of the bad publicity, so I brought her here to this private hospital." Devon runs his fingers through his hair. He's shifting his stance. I can tell there's something he's not telling me. "They're very...discreet here."

"I want to see my sister. Now."

Devon grabs my arm, and the way he's looking deeply into my eyes makes me very nervous. Something is terribly wrong.

"I'm going to warn you, Norah doesn't look good. She suffered from oxygen deprivation and has burns on the left side of her body. Right now we're not sure how much damage there was to her brain, but it looks like she has a long recovery ahead of her."

I haven't even seen my sister yet, and I already feel like I'm going to burst into tears.

When I walk into the room, it's hard to believe that's my sister on the bed. There are about a half dozen beeping monitors connected to her. Most of her body is covered in bandages, and about half of them look like they have fluid oozing through them.

I walk closer. Her face wasn't burnt, but she's just staring at the wall. At first I think maybe she's watching TV. I step between her and the TV, but she doesn't react. I wave my hands, but she still doesn't respond.

"Norah, it's me," I say. Her green eyes are still there, but the fire inside is gone.

A young female nurse walks into the room. "Is there a doctor I can speak to?" My voice shakes as I speak. I'm on the verge of tears.

"I'll get the doctor now." The nurse turns on her heel and walks out of the room.

29

The next morning, Devon and I meet at a local café just down the street from the hospital. I struggled to sleep last night as I grappled with my sister's condition. The doctor wasn't full of hope for Norah's recovery. I've been trying to process all the emotions. Mostly, I feel guilty for leaving Norah.

Would this have happened if I had stayed?

When I'm not grappling with the guilt, I feel anger. I mean, who would have done this to my sister? How did she get caught in the fire? Devon didn't give me a lot of details.

So as soon as I woke, I untangled myself from Luis's arms and pulled on some clothes. I shot off a message to Devon.

Can we meet?

I brushed my teeth and washed my face as I waited for his response.

Sure. Meet me at this café in fifteen minutes.

Then he sent a pin of the location.

I arrive a few minutes late, huffing from the walk across the city blocks. Devon is waiting for me outside the café. As I approach the small bistro table, I see him before he sees me. His shoulders are hunched over his phone. He looks somehow smaller than when I left. This whole situation must be taking a toll on him.

Do I feel sorry for him? I'm still undecided. It depends how much he had to do with this whole debacle my sister is in.

I sit down across from him.

"I ordered you a cappuccino, two sugars."

"Thanks." I gingerly take the cup. "I'm surprised you remembered."

He shrugs and attempts a weak smile. Devon is traditionally handsome—blue eyes, a full head of hair, a strong jaw—but today he looks tired. He's lost weight, which emphasizes the dark circles under his eyes. His normally clean-shaven beard is long and scruffy.

"Has she really been like this for three months?"

He nods. "The doctors have told me that, at this point, she has very little chance of recovery."

I look down at my cup. It's the same prognosis the doctor gave me yesterday.

"So what, she's just going to stare off into space forever?" I ask, looking back at Devon.

"From what the doctors are telling me? Yes." He takes a small sip of his coffee. As he sets down the cup, I see his wedding ring catch the light. "I never imagined this would happen."

"Devon, I'm sorry." Despite what I thought of Devon before I left, he seems to have stuck by my sister.

"Tell me more about what happened the night of the fire," I say.

Devon takes a long breath. Looks down. "There's not a lot to tell. I was on my way home from the restaurant. Norah stayed behind. She wanted to try a new soufflé recipe." He brushes his hands through his hair. "I took the subway. My cell service is patchy down there. By the time I arrived in the Lower East Side twenty minutes later, I had half a dozen missed calls. One from the fire department. I took a cab, got there as fast as I could."

His eyes mist over. He swallows. "They had pulled Norah out by the time I got there. But she was burned badly. I made a few calls. She went to the emergency room first. Then as soon as she was stable enough, we brought her here."

My stomach twists in knots as he tells me the story. "You don't know what started the fire?"

"The fire marshal said it likely started near the oven," he says, looking at me. His eyes are clear again. "But other than that, no." His expression changes. "Naomi, there's something more I need to tell you."

I stare at him for a moment, not sure if I want to hear what he has to say.

"Okay, what?"

"After you left, the bills, they just kept piling up. They raised our rent at the restaurant, the building needed renovations, and we had to bring on new staff." Devon runs a hand through his hair. "Even though we were successful, I was struggling to keep up with the bills. At that point we had maximized all of the bank loans we could get." He clears his throat. "So I reached out to a client of mine from the old law office. He connected me with some people who could loan us the money we needed to expand the space. Off the books."

Devon looks down at his cup, fumbling with the paper sleeve. "I thought there was no way we wouldn't be able to pay him back. I mean, we had a reservation list for six months out."

"So you borrowed money from the wrong people," I say.

"Yes," says Devon. Our eyes meet again, and I notice a touch of shame in his expression.

This is not good news. I remember Norah saying something about how Devon liked to play outside the rules.

"But the restaurant was successful; there was a reservation waiting list a mile long..."

"Sure, we were busy. But we had so much debt from the build-out, the lease, not to mention the rise in the cost of food." He shakes his head. "We just couldn't get ahead."

Or you're just bad with money. I chew the inside of my cheek. But this isn't the time to pick a fight. Clearly the money is already gone.

"What about the insurance money from the fire? Could you use that to pay them back?"

He pulls at the collar of his shirt, looking away from me.

"There is no insurance money."

My mouth goes dry. "Why?"

Devon shifts in his seat. "Like I said, the fire marshal thinks it started near the oven. But no one knows for sure." His eyes dart to the side. "They haven't ruled out arson."

I suck in a breath. *Arson?* Someone set the restaurant on fire on purpose? And almost killed my sister? My entire body goes rigid.

"Who would do that?" I ask, my voice shaking.

"I don't know." Devon shakes his head. "I also don't know if it was really arson, or if it was just an accident. Like I said, they're still investigating. Regardless, the insurance company says that until the investigation is over, they can't give us any money."

"So how do we pay for her care?" I ask. "Does she need to be in a facility? A nursing home? What do people do in this situation?"

Devon leans back heavily on his seat and lets out a breath. "I'm trying to figure that out right now. She will need a nurse to check in on her. But not twenty-four-hour care."

I get the feeling there's more.

"Devon, are you sure you're telling me everything?" The two of us lock eyes. This man is now in charge of my sister for the rest of her life. But if he had something to do with that fire, I will jump across this table and strangle him.

He holds my gaze. "Naomi, I had nothing to do with the fire. I'm telling you everything I know."

I'm sure Devon is a good liar. I'm sure he lied about things to my sister. Maybe he's lying right now. But I don't have much choice. I have to trust him. I sigh.

"Okay," I say. "So don't you just file for bankruptcy? Or call the police?"

Devon leans forward. "The guys I owe money to? Those guys don't care if you're bankrupt or not." He pauses. "And you definitely don't want to go to the police. They, um, know people who work for the police."

A silence hangs between us for a moment as he lets that settle in. I'm speechless. It feels like a bad situation that keeps getting worse.

"There's one more thing I need to tell you."

I sit in silence, holding my breath. What could possibly be any worse than what he just told me?

"If the guys I owe money to don't get the money from me, they may come after you."

I feel my body go slack. "Me, why?"

"Don't you remember? You're one-third owner of Pepper. So this isn't just about me and Norah anymore. This is about you too."

I could kill my brother-in-law right now. But that won't do any good. I shake my head.

"How much money do we owe?"

Devon licks his lips. "Seven hundred and fifty thousand."

My stomach drops. I'm speechless.

"That's why I need your help," he says.

I push away my coffee. "Well, I got news for you, brother-in-law. If money is what you're looking for, I don't have any. The money I made on the yacht isn't going to put a dent in that."

Devon places his elbows on the table, clasping his hands in front of him. He lowers his voice. "It's not the money that I need. I need a new star. I need a new restaurant. And most of all, I need Norah."

I furrow my brow. "Norah is obviously not in any condition to cook."

Devon sits back in his chair. "Naomi, has anyone ever told you how much you and Norah look alike?"

Every day of my life when we were kids.

"Yes, why?"

"I bet if we cut your hair and dyed it dark brown, you would look exactly like her. You could even wear green contacts. Everyone would assume you were her."

I feel stunned, letting the gravity of his suggestion settle in my belly. It's clear from the dark circles under his eyes, Devon hasn't been sleeping well. I think the lack of sleep might be affecting his logic.

"So what, you want me to dress up as my sister and play chef? Devon, that's absurd."

"I know it sounds ridiculous, but these guys I owe money to...? If I don't get a new up-and-coming restaurant together and make them believe I'm going to pay them back..." His face goes slightly pale. "I don't even want to think about what they would do to me."

He looks deep into my eyes. "Or to you for that matter."

I feel a sinking sensation settle in my stomach.

"What you're suggesting is insane. It would never work."

"Why not? No one knows Norah is here. No one but you, me and Luis."

I chew on my lip. He has a point. But there are so many details he's overlooking.

"What about the news? Did they cover the fire?"

Devon taps the table. "I had some help keeping things quiet. So while the news ran with the story of the fire, Norah's injuries were not mentioned."

"Help from who?"

"The investors we owe the money to."

I roll my eyes and slump into my chair. Clearly he's thought this through. Devon might be shady, but he's not anybody's fool.

"Okay, maybe I could pass for my sister. But what about cooking? I don't cook. I'm not a chef. I don't have the talent Norah has."

"I have all of Norah's recipes." He points to a briefcase leaning against his seat. "Notebooks full of ideas. We just need someone who could work closely with you. Someone we can share our secret with, someone who can make you look like a chef. And then together we can launch a new restaurant."

Immediately, I think of Luis. But before I open my mouth, I hesitate. *Do I really want to bring him into this?*

"Let's say this crazy plan would actually work. I make everyone believe I'm Norah. How are you going to find the money to launch a new restaurant, and where would you put it? You already told me that the places in New York are way too expensive."

Devon pulls out his phone. "Here," he says. The photo he shows me is of a quaint little farm surrounded by wildflowers. A large bank-style barn is in the background, with a small creek running around the front.

"That's a farm," I say.

"Have I ever told you about my family's estate that's located in Maine? It's about an hour outside of Portland in a new up-and-coming area of restaurants. I think with the right publicity we could make it one of the hottest destinations in the Northeast."

"Maine?"

"Yes. Trust me, I think this could really work. It's all I've been thinking about for the last few months. Once the insurance money comes through, we can pay our debts, and you'll be free to do whatever you want."

That gut feeling returns again. The same one I felt the first time I met Devon. He scratches the stubble on his cheek, studying me.

"We're meeting with my investors tomorrow night. I'll pick you up at nine o'clock," he says.

"I don't know..."

Devon reaches over and places his hand on my arm. I flinch at his touch.

"I need you to fully commit to this, Naomi. I know you're a free spirit. I know you don't like staying in one place for too long." He pulls his hand away and touches his temple.

"But if we don't pull this off? We'll both be dead."

30

"Where are we going?" I say to Devon as we pull off the interstate. We've been driving for about an hour, crossing from the city limits out to the suburbs. We pass rows and rows of housing complexes. And then finally we reach some open land. It's pitch black out here, and I suddenly feel unsure of my decision to come.

"We're here," Devon says as we pull up to a large security gate. I look out the window and see a large square sign that says Providence Storage.

"What are we doing at a storage facility?" I ask.

"My investors run a large storage operation," he says as he rolls down the window. "The main income comes from storage facilities all along the East Coast. And, of course, they pursue other more high-risk investments, like Pepper."

He reaches his hand out the window and pushes a metal intercom button. "Devon Winthrop," he says. A few seconds later I hear a beep, and the gates swing open.

As we pull in, I see a long line of expensive vehicles, from

Mercedes to BMWs. *The storage business must be doing pretty well.* Devon pulls into a spot near the front door of a gray warehouse building.

As we step out of the vehicle and onto the concrete, I get an uneasy feeling that clenches my stomach. It's dark out here, and there are very few lights, casting long shadows along the buildings. There's a barbed-wire fence that rattles in the wind as we walk to the front door.

We're completely alone, and the only person I can trust is my not-so-trustworthy brother-in-law.

"Are you sure about this?" I peer over at Devon in the darkness.

"I promise everything will be fine." He takes a step closer to me as we near the front door. "Just follow my lead."

My heart beats a little bit faster as he pulls open the door, and we step inside.

What I expect to see is a long hall with storage lockers on each side. Just like the one where Luis and I stored our belongings during the yacht trip.

But that's not what we walk into. There are rows of square LED lights that line the ceiling, long leather couches, pool tables, and a large bar that runs along the right side of the room. It feels almost like a fancy Manhattan clubhouse rather than a storage building out in the middle of the suburbs.

Before I can open my mouth to ask Devon about the space, a tall man with striking white hair approaches us.

"Devon, you made it," he says. He's wearing a fitted suit with a pair of expensive-looking Gucci loafers and a large diamond pinky ring. As soon as he approaches us, I feel the hairs on the back of my arms stand up.

"Anthony," Devon says, reaching out to grasp his hand,

"thanks for meeting with us." The man looks at me expectantly. "I'd like you to meet my sister-in-law, Naomi. Naomi, this is Anthony Bello."

Anthony rests his gray eyes on mine. He reaches out his hand to me, which I take. When I try to pull away, he gently resists.

"Naomi, I am so sorry to hear about your sister," he says. "We had hoped she would recover."

I say nothing, just nod. When he finally lets go of my hand, which is now sweaty, I resist the urge to wipe it on my pants.

"Let's go ahead and meet in my office in the back," he says, gesturing to a set of large double doors at the back of the room.

As the two of us walk behind him, I take in the rest of the room. There are a couple of dozen people, both men and women, spread out across the room. They all appear to be having a good time, drinking and playing pool. The men are dressed mostly in suits, while the women wear what I would describe as cocktail dresses. The whole environment gives me a sick feeling, like I shouldn't be here.

The three of us step into Anthony's office, which, much like the rest of the space, is fully decorated with an expensive-looking plush carpet and leather furniture.

Anthony walks around the room and sits behind a large banker's desk.

"Please have a seat," he says, gesturing to the two leather chairs across from his desk.

As we settle into the chairs, a woman enters the room and presents each of us with an ice-cold martini.

"Please have a drink," Anthony says.

I hesitate for a moment, looking sideways at Devon. He

raises his eyebrows at me and takes a sip. I follow suit, the liquid burning my throat.

"So, Devon," Anthony says, setting down his glass, "have you discussed with Naomi her role in launching the new restaurant in Maine?"

Devon takes a drink from his glass before answering.

"I have," he says. He looks over at me. "She's open to the idea, but I don't think she's quite convinced."

My mouth goes dry.

"I have to say, the resemblance between you and your sister is striking," Anthony says.

I'm not sure what to say. This was a decision I had hoped to make in private. I confessed everything to Luis, and he was eager to help. But as I look around the room, I don't think there's any way I can bring him into this.

What was my sister thinking? Did she know about all of this?

Anthony leans back in his leather chair, which creaks under the weight of his body. The music from the club room behind us gently thumps into the office. But I hear another sound coming from a large door in the corner. It almost sounds as if someone is grunting during a hard workout.

But then a sound comes from the room that makes my heart beat a little bit faster, my shoulders tense, and my stomach drop to the floor. It sounds as if somebody's being punched in the face.

Anthony is watching me.

"I'm sorry, Naomi, we have some business that's being taken care of in the back room." He takes a drink from his glass, and the diamond ring on his pinky catches the light.

Business? That doesn't sound like any business transaction I've ever been a part of.

"You see, when we invest in one of our more risky

ventures, things don't always go as planned." He glances over at Devon. "But as long as our associates are reasonable, we are reasonable."

I hear a scream come from the room, and I nearly drop my glass.

"But when our associates are not reasonable," he continues, "we have to take things to the next level in order to protect our investment." He takes another drink and looks at me with his cold, gray eyes. I'm holding my breath. "Make sense?"

I reach forward and set my glass down on the table. "Yes," I croak.

He smiles at me, reminding me of the Cheshire cat. "Good," he says. "Now, let's get down to business. Devon says that you are open to the idea of opening the restaurant and that you'd be happy to"—he pauses and looks up at the ceiling, then back at me—"fill in for your sister, Norah. Is there anything we can do to persuade you to say yes?"

Devon and Anthony are both looking at me. I shift in my seat. Sweat is pooling under my arms. *Do I have a choice?*

"I'm sure we could work it out," I say. I reach for my drink, taking a small sip.

"Excellent," he says, sitting up in his seat. "You see, I was thinking that your friend Luis would be a great sous chef."

At this point, I choke on the martini, coughing. I spill a bit of it down my front and on my lap. Anthony puts down his glass, pulls a blue pocket square from his jacket and hands it to me.

"Here, take this," he says. I dab the liquid on the white blouse I'm wearing and then the corners of my mouth before handing the pocket square back to him.

"No, you keep it," he says. I fold it in my hand, noticing it has his initials embroidered on the corner, then take a breath, clearing my throat.

"How do you know about Luis?" I ask. His eyes flicker to Devon.

"Oh, Devon mentioned his name. In fact, we met Luis outside your hotel just an hour ago. One of my men was passing by and recognized him from a photo that Devon shared with us."

I give Devon a sharp look. He simply takes another sip of his martini. It's all I can do not to reach over and scratch his eyes out. *How could he?*

"We also took a look at his excellent résumé and realized that Luis doesn't have his green card yet, which is a shame. Did you know Luis comes from a very dangerous town in Guatemala that's run by a drug cartel?"

I swallow. Luis mentioned he came from a dangerous place. And he swore he'd never go back.

"Yes," I say.

"Well, it would be terrible for him to return. But I know some people who can help us."

I'm so angry at Devon right now I could scream. I grip the arms of the chair until my knuckles are white.

"As for you? Well, you know when we signed on to invest with Pepper, your name was on the list of guarantors," he says. "So you are already indebted to us. And like I said, it's better when our associates work with us so that we don't have to take matters to the next level."

As if on cue, I hear a loud and painful-sounding groan from the other room. I nearly jump out of my seat. Then there's a sharp knock on the door. I hold my breath. The door cracks open, and a large man in a white button-down shirt with his sleeves rolled up peeks into the room. I notice he has a little bit of blood and bruising on his knuckles.

"Excuse me, sir," says the man.

"Yes?" Anthony looks over but doesn't get up from his seat.

"We've settled negotiations. Our driver is returning him home."

"Thank you," Anthony says. He takes another sip of his drink, clearly relishing our discomfort.

The man nods and closes the door. I feel light-headed, like I might pass out.

"Well, I'd better let you two get to work," Anthony says as he stands up. "By the way, I had an idea for the name of the restaurant."

"Oh, what's that?" says Devon.

"I thought you might call it Thistle. I know that they grow wild in Maine, and I always liked the prickly leaves. They draw just a bit of blood. It's a pretty smart plant that learns how to protect itself, don't you think?"

I swallow. Devon cocks his head to the side.

"I like that," he says. "I think we'll keep it."

31

ONE YEAR AGO

"I don't think I can do this anymore," I say to Devon. The two of us are sitting inside his office on the Winthrop estate.

There isn't a place in the world I hate more than this small, wood-paneled room. Devon spent a small fortune putting in custom skylights in the ceiling. One entire wall of the space is lined in custom bookcases too, which house a bunch of law books, restaurant awards, and a few photos. If you push on one of the shelves, the whole panel opens up to a small room where Devon has a large safe full of money. That's one of the things about Thistle, we don't have the greatest internet signal to run credit cards out here, so we always suggest our customers come with cash.

It's crossed my mind several times to just steal the cash and make a run for it. But I could never leave my sister.

The irony of it is that in order to get into the room, you have to move a photo of the three of us—Norah, Devon, and me—standing in front of Pepper. I always thought it strange he kept that photo of us in public.

But then, no one has any reason to believe I'm not Norah Winthrop.

"What do you mean, Naomi?" he says, stroking his chin. "You're doing great. Everything is going just as we planned."

It's going great for *him*. He's the one making bank. Supposedly he's building a fund for Norah's care. But lately, with the way he's been spending money on this place, I doubt there's anything left. The other thing he has? Maybe the thing he covets the most?

Control.

He has complete control over me and Luis. He's made that clear. If I leave? He turns me over to his "investors." And if Luis leaves? Anthony has already made it clear that any chance of getting his green card will disappear. And then Luis will be on a direct flight back to Guatemala.

So yeah, it's going great for Devon Winthrop.

"The restaurant is running so well now," I say. "Why can't you find someone to replace me?"

I know the answer, but I want to hear it from him. He loosens the tie on his suit and starts to remove it.

"Because people come here to see Norah Winthrop, former owner of Pepper. Chef extraordinaire." He sets the tie on his desk. "If there's no Norah, there's no business. And if there's no business, that means no money. And if there's no money? You know what that means."

All the muscles in my body tense. I slam my hand down on his desk.

"What? So I'm supposed to just spend the rest of my life pretending to be my sister?"

"No, Naomi," he says, his expression neutral. "Just until we pay them back. It will take another year, tops."

"I can't last another year."

He purses his lips together. "We don't have a choice. We're in too deep now."

"Where's all the money going, anyway? And where do we stand with the insurance?"

"I'm still waiting to hear back. It could be any day now." He shrugs. "But I wouldn't count on them. Besides, as soon as we finish renovating the cabins and open the boutique hotel rooms around the lake, the money will really start rolling in."

I roll my eyes. I've heard this song and dance about the "boutique hotel" before.

"I don't think you want to pay off Anthony and his goons. I think you like working with him."

"Like I said, we don't have a choice." He glowers at me.

"We could run. We could start over somewhere else," I say, leaning forward.

"Now why would we do that? We have everything we need here."

I stare at him, trying to think of what to say. There has to be a way out of this. I let the breath leave my chest. He's right. I don't have a choice. Neither does Luis.

After I told Luis about the meeting at the storage warehouse, I begged him to leave and go back to Florida. But he refused to leave me.

Now we're both stuck.

"Okay, one more year. But after that? I'm gone for good."

Devon leans forward. "You know this isn't just about the money, right?" he says, staring at me intently. "This is about her too. If there's no money, then there's no nurse and no place for her to live. What you have to understand is—if I go down, there will be no one to care for her."

Of course I feel terrible for my sister. I can't believe the position she's in, and the worst part? She hasn't gotten any better. She still just sits there all day, staring, while we bring her food to feed her. The nurse comes in through the back road of the property each day to care for her.

But what kind of life is that? What kind of life is it just to do nothing?

"What about the experimental trial? The one I found in Florida. I talked to the doctor, and they said they could take her—"

"I've told you before, Naomi, we can't afford it. Not yet."

I throw my hands up. "I don't get it, Devon. How can you afford top-of-the-line equipment here at Thistle, but you can't afford to give my sister a chance for the future?"

Devon leans forward in his seat, anger flashing in his eyes.

"Do you think I don't care about her?"

I have my doubts.

But I don't say so. Instead, the two of us stare at each other for a moment, like a couple of lions in the wild getting ready to attack. A thought that has floated around in my mind for the last couple of years finally makes its way to my mouth.

I blink, breaking our silence. "Devon, I've been wondering, do you have life insurance?"

Devon gives me a hard look. "Yes, why?"

"Oh, no reason, it was just something I was looking into for Luis and me. You know, in case anything ever happens to me, I want him to be taken care of."

Devon grinds his teeth. "I don't know what you mean by that, Naomi. But if you're threatening me—"

"I would never threaten you, Devon," I say. "We're in this together, remember?" I get up from my seat. "I have to get back to the kitchen. To make sure this restaurant will run smoothly."

Devon says nothing, just watches as I walk out the door.

As I make my way from his office in the milk house back to the main building, an idea forms in my mind. Devon isn't going to let me off the hook anytime soon, if ever. I love my sister, but playing house with her husband isn't going to bring her back. Or get her the help she needs.

I'm going to run it by Luis tonight. But the main idea is this—I need to find a replacement for Norah, or Devon is never going to let me leave.

32

THREE MONTHS AGO

I tap the end of my blunt chocolate bob, which has just been freshly lopped off by a local hairstylist. I call it the Norah cut. I remember the first time I had it styled this way. The stylist swiveled the salon chair around, and I stared in the mirror. My jaw dropped.

Devon was right. With a few changes, I look exactly like my sister. I remember going back to my bedroom and pulling out an article about Pepper. I went to the bathroom and held up the magazine next to my face. Our faces, a combination of our parents' features, were nearly identical. I shivered. It was a bit creepy, even if she is my sister.

Truthfully, I'm so sick of this haircut. As soon as I leave this place, I plan to shave it all off. Not to mention the contacts. As Devon pointed out a little over a year ago, one of the prime differences between Norah and me is in the eyes. While my true eye color is a hazel gray, Norah has striking pale green eyes. In order to pull off this charade, I had to get green contacts. Devon had them custom made.

I've never worn contacts in my whole life. I have perfect vision. So the contacts have been an adjustment as well. Really it's a culmination of all of it—the hair, the attitude, the food. Being my sister is exhausting.

Don't get me wrong. I love food. I love to eat. But being a highly rated chef? It's less about the food and more about the art. It's about perfection. I don't have the patience for that level of perfection...that was Norah's thing.

There's a part of me that's proud of what I have accomplished. I never went to acting school, but pretending to be someone else is not easy. Even if you've known that person your entire life. Devon and I made sure that no one from Pepper got a job here. We couldn't risk it, even if they had the talent and the desire to work here. And our old VIP guests? We left them off the guest list too. Even interviews were limited to new journalists only.

We've been careful. And it's working. No one seems to suspect a thing. Not a whisper or a suggestion that Norah Winthrop is anyone but who they expect her to be. But it's time to let Norah go and put all this behind me.

Luis and I have been lying in bed late at night, talking about what the future looks like for us. The first thing I can tell you is that we won't be running a restaurant together. That's going to be buried in the past. If I never have to look at a cutting board or sauté pan again in my life, I'll be happy. It'll be carryout for me for at least a year. I'll take a greasy meal at McDonald's over any restaurant owned by Devon Winthrop. Some of our plans include backpacking through Europe, maybe hiking in the Himalayan mountains, or traveling to Japan.

Anywhere but Maine.

Devon was right when we first discussed this plan. It's hard for me to stay in one place for so long. I'm itching to get out, see the world.

Devon seems happy to stay here. Although I use the term "happy" loosely with him. His mental state seems to be deteriorating. He's been drinking more. He falls into fits of anger, where he lashes out at the staff. Maybe he feels bad about my sister. Or maybe it's stress. I don't know. In fact, there's been a few times when he's actually lashed out at me, and it's weird to see the same bruises on my arms that Norah had before I left on the yacht.

It took everything Luis had not to rip Devon's head off when he saw what Devon had done to me. But Devon has control over him too. If Luis pushes Devon too far? He will have him deported.

So today I've put on a fresh black shirt just like Norah always used to wear. I've got her haircut. I have my contacts. I'm wearing the gold best-friend necklace I gave her in high school. I'm playing my part to the fullest for the next few days of interviews for our new dishwasher.

At least, Devon thinks I'm hiring a dishwasher. What I'm really looking for is my replacement.

I have a table set up in the dining room with a white tablecloth, flowers, and two glasses of water. I requested to have all the lights on in the room, including the sparkling chandeliers, so I can get a good view of the candidates. I've also asked Ingrid to keep the staff away so my attention is fully focused on the interviews. She might think my requests are strange, but Ingrid's never been one to ask questions.

My first interview of the day is a young woman named Sadie Jackson. I've read over her résumé a dozen times, which includes some experience at Château Bernard. I have a few connections there, as I used to work with a guy named Peter at one of the restaurants in New York.

Well, Naomi worked with Peter.

He acted a little strange when I phoned him for more details. But I kept peeling back the layers. He finally admitted they'd had a relationship. And that she never worked in the kitchen, only as a waitress. Although he was quick to point out that he'd tasted her cooking and she has talent.

It was then I knew she was perfect.

From what I knew of Peter, he only dated beautiful women. So she had to be pretty. And the other important part? She'd lied on her résumé, which tells me another thing about Sadie Jackson. She's comfortable with a moral gray area, which is a necessity to work here.

A person who has a squeaky-clean background might run at the first sight of how things are handled here at Thistle.

So before I even meet her, I assume she's desperate, beautiful, and talented. Which checks all the boxes. Of course, I'll still make her sweat before I give her the job, but I am cautiously optimistic that Sadie Jackson is the key to my future.

When she walks in the door with her curvy body, full lips, blue eyes, and soft blonde hair, my jaw almost drops. She's gorgeous. And young. As I conduct the interview, it becomes obvious that she's desperate to work here. That she worships Norah Winthrop. That she'll do anything to please me. And that she's exactly the type of person Devon will fall for.

I plan on keeping a careful distance from her, just like the rest of the staff. I'm afraid if anyone gets too close, they'll figure out I'm not some famous chef from New York.

In fact, it's better if she hates me. That way she won't feel bad about stealing my husband.

33

ONE WEEK AGO

"Norah, wait!"

Devon is yelling my name through the dark as I walk back to my sister's cabin. Everything is going to plan. Sadie is turning out even better than I thought she would. She's hardworking, talented. I can tell that Devon is attracted to her.

Tonight was a turning point. I let Sadie create a dish for me. It was perfect—a puffed pastry with an ice-cream quenelle. I discussed it with Luis, who agreed it was well balanced and delicious. Even the presentation was well executed. It was a rush when the food hit my lips. I knew in that moment that she could pull it off. She could replace me.

But I wanted to keep her hungry to please, so I pulled it from the menu. And then she pulled that little stunt in the hallway where she threatened to tell Devon about me and Luis. *The irony.*

I turn around to face Devon. Of course, I want the idea of me leaving to be his. So, initially, I can't act like I'm happy that Sadie is taking my place.

"So she's my replacement, huh? You think she can hack it? Make you enough money to pay back those mobsters you're working with?"

"Keep your voice down," he says, trying to catch up with me.

"If I go, you know Luis will follow me," I say.

"I wouldn't be so sure about that, Norah."

"Not everything is about money, Devon," I say in a harsh whisper. I quickly untie my apron strings and rip it off my waist. "I quit." I shove the cloth apron into his chest.

"You can't quit. You know that," he says.

"Or what? You'll stop caring for her? She'd be better off in a nursing home than stuck in that shitty little cabin."

"You know we can't afford—"

"Well, you'd better figure out how. Because I'm done playing chef," I say.

"Wait!" he cries. I keep walking. "Norah, we need to talk. There's more at stake here."

I turn around to face him. He takes a few long strides forward, crossing the distance of a few feet between us.

"You know my name is not Norah."

We're standing on the crushed limestone path between the restaurant kitchen and some of the farm buildings on the east side of the property. I shiver from the cold air.

"Come on, please, let's talk in my office." He nods his head toward the old barn where he keeps his office.

I roll my eyes. "Fine."

We walk in silence toward the office building. The tension hangs in the air between us. I'm running the conversation we're about to have through my head. One that I've rehearsed with Luis over and over.

Devon arrives at the doorway and yanks the door open for me.

We walk into his office. He spent a small fortune on the woodworking, not to mention the giant mahogany desk in the center of the room. I clench my fists. Just the sight of it infuriates me. All I can see is money that could've been saved for my sister's care. Had he saved the money instead of spending it on his lavish office, he would probably have almost enough money to pay for her medical trial treatment. But it's clear to me that Devon has no desire for my sister to get better.

"Have a seat, Naomi," he says through clenched teeth. I take a seat in the chair across from him, and he flops into the desk chair.

"What is going on with you lately?" he asks as he reaches over and pours himself a bourbon. He offers me a glass. I shake my head.

"I'm done, Devon. I want out."

"As I've told you before, Naomi, there's no way out. Not yet. We have to make this work."

"I think you're wrong," I say. I'm sitting on pins and needles. My hands sweat. "Things have changed here."

He takes a sip of his drink. "How so?"

"Sadie," I say. Devon raises his eyebrows. I take a deep breath. This is my chance to sell him on my idea. I don't want to mess it up. "Don't you see? She's what you need to take Thistle to the next level. She's a talented chef. A hard worker. Not to mention she's beautiful. And she loves her work."

I steady myself as I utter the next words. "She's even better than Norah."

Even as I say the words, it feels like a betrayal. My sister was the best. I'll never live up to her talent. And, honestly, neither will Sadie.

And I really don't like Sadie. Which is good, because it's made this whole thing a little easier. I think she's an opportunist, and I think at any moment she would jump in bed with my brother-in-law. But it doesn't matter how I feel about her. It only matters that she can take my place.

Devon takes a swig of his expensive whiskey and pours another. It takes everything in me not to reach over and slap it out of his hand.

He rubs his chin as he looks at me. I can tell the wheels are turning.

"Why do I need Sadie when I have you?"

"Haven't you seen the reviews lately? We've plateaued. We've gotten as much publicity for this place as we can," I say. Which is all true, depending on how you look at it. "With the cabins opening next year, you need a new star. You need someone who makes a splash across the culinary world."

I pause for a moment, letting him picture Sadie's pretty face next to him on the latest *Bon Appétit* cover.

"Me? I'm old news. Norah Winthrop is old news. And that's why we didn't get the second Michelin star."

Devon makes a face. I've hit a sour note with him. Despite his every effort to pay off any Michelin inspector he can get his hands on, we didn't get the second star. Luis and I were the ones who made sure of that. We downgraded Norah's recipes just enough to make sure we didn't get selected.

"The kitchen you've built here is flawless," I continue. "But people are going to start wondering—where are all the new recipes? Did you see the article in *Taste* last week? The one where the critic wondered why we're serving the same dishes we did at Pepper?"

Devon breathes deeply and leans back into his chair. *He knows I'm right.* He squints at me as the glass hangs in his hand. I keep going.

"And you can't deny that you're attracted to her," I say.

Devon makes a huffing noise. "I'm married. *To your sister.*"

I throw up my hands. "Oh, come on, Devon. Like that's ever stopped you before." I'm pretty sure he's slept with a few of the hostesses. But I've never said a word. Devon scowls at me.

I shrug. "I can't blame you. The old Norah is gone. You've been alone the last few years."

Devon sits up in his seat and places his glass on the desk. The wheels are turning now. My plan is working.

"Okay, so let's say you're right. Let's say that Sadie can take over here and give me what I need. A new star." He licks his lips. "What do I tell everybody about my wife?"

"You get divorced," I say. "At least on paper. Luis and I will disappear. I'll come back for Norah as soon as I save enough money for us to have a place. We'll change our names. You'll never see us again."

Devon furrows his brows. "It's a huge risk."

I feel a wave of courage rise up inside me. I grip the sides of the chair and lean forward.

"It's a bigger risk to keep me here. Eventually, someone is going to find out."

"How?"

I raise my eyebrows.

"As I've told you before, Naomi, don't threaten me."

"I'm not threatening you, Devon. I'm giving you the

opportunity to do the right thing and make the best career move all at the same time."

The two of us stare at each other across the desk for what feels like an eternity. I've laid out my plans as best I can, but it's still up to Devon whether we leave or not. I hold my breath.

"Okay," Devon says. "I'll let you go, but until the money is paid off, your third of the money, Norah stays here with me."

My stomach tightens. "Fine."

"And if you screw me over on this? Norah might not be so well taken care of."

Heat rises up to my neck, ears, and cheeks. It's all I can do not to jump across the table and strangle him. I can't believe he's threatening to hurt my sister after all this time.

"Fine," I say through clenched teeth. "You have a deal."

I stand up and extend my hand, which is trembling slightly. Devon also stands and shakes it, but instead of letting go, he pulls me toward him.

"Just remember, Naomi. If I go down?" He squeezes my hand so hard that I almost yell out in pain. "I'm taking you, your boyfriend, and your sister down with me."

PART III

PRESENT DAY

34

SADIE

It's Thursday morning, my first day as head chef. I find myself staring in the mirror, barely able to move. I splash a little water on my face and look again. But let's face it, there is no way to erase what I saw last night. The dark circles under my eyes remind me of that.

After I saw Norah, or whatever version of Norah that was, I ran. I ran like a terrified child through the dark all the way back to my cabin. When I arrived safely inside, I shut the door and locked it, then crawled into bed, under the covers. As if whatever I just saw would disappear like a bad dream.

But it wasn't a bad dream.

I tried to fall asleep, which, of course, was futile. Should I jump out of bed and run to Devon's house and ask him what the heck is going on? I almost did, several times. But something in my gut told me I needed time to think about it. So I just lay there in my bed, staring at the ceiling.

The image of Norah in the cabin is seared into my brain. The vacant, empty stare. As if she is no longer in there. Her hair is cut the same, although slightly longer than the pictures I've seen of her. Her eyes were still the same pale shade of green.

But she was gone. And when I waved my hands in front of her, she didn't even see me. My mind reeled with the possibilities. Was she on drugs? Why was she here? It was difficult to process what I was seeing.

I noticed she had burn marks that ran from her left hand all the way up to her neck. The fire at Pepper. This had to have something to do with the fire. But how?

And who the heck is pretending to be Norah Winthrop?

I know I have to confront Devon. Even if it means giving up my dream. My dream of seeing the menu I created come to life. I'm also terrified of knowing the truth.

A few hours later, I pull my hair back, don my chef's coat, and step out into the crisp Maine air. It sends a chill through my body. My body trembles, trying to adapt to the drop in temperature.

I march across the property straight to Devon's office. I knock on the door, and Devon opens it. Of course, he looks as handsome as ever. He's already dressed, in a pale beige cashmere sweater and jeans. I swallow.

"Sadie! Good morning," he says and leans in to kiss me on the lips. I return the kiss, but keep it brief. He pulls away and looks at me. "Is everything okay?"

"We need to talk," I say, moving past him into the office. He closes the door behind me, then takes a seat at his desk and gestures for me to sit down across from him.

"What's going on?"

"Something happened." My voice shakes as I speak. "I mean, I found something."

Devon looks at me, a confused look on his face. "It's okay. Take your time," he says.

Thoughts are racing through my mind so quickly I have trouble getting the right words out.

"I...well, I went to the cabin last night. The cabin at the back of the lake."

I'm not sure exactly how I expect Devon to react. I don't know if he's going to be surprised, or maybe take a sharp breath. Or maybe I think he'll be mad at me.

Instead, Devon looks at me, and his expression doesn't change at all.

"So you found Norah," he says. I nod.

I stare at him for a moment, waiting for him to explain. He leans back in his chair.

"I planned on telling you tonight, actually, after your first shift as head chef." He shrugs. "But now is as good a time as any."

My heart is literally racing as he speaks.

"As you know, there was a fire at Pepper. What I haven't told you—and honestly, what I haven't told anyone—is that Norah was injured in the fire. She suffered extensive burns on the left side of her body. She also suffered from oxygen deprivation."

His posture changes. A look of deep sadness settles into his face.

"At first, we hoped she might get better. I set her up in a private hospital in New York. We had doctors, nurses, and therapists working with her daily. Her burns healed, but..." He stares off for a moment. "Her brain never recovered. After months and months of therapy, we realized she wasn't going to get any better. That she would need care for the rest of her life. I had to accept there was no chance that she was coming back."

"So she's just going to stay like that forever? Just staring into space?"

He nods his head softly. His eyes moisten.

"I know it's not the greatest quality of life. Since the fire, I've been working to make enough money to get her into an experimental trial in Florida. It might be another year or two, but I've been saving up enough money so that she can get more help. And maybe even get some of her memories and her cognitive ability back."

I take this into consideration. A question flashes in my mind. *Where do I stand if Norah comes back?*

I shake my head. The real question that's been gnawing at me is what I ask next.

"Who in the world is the Norah Winthrop I've been working for over the last three months?"

Devon's eyes move across the room. Regardless of what he says next, I already have my answer.

35

SADIE

I turn my head, my eyes tracing the wooden bookcase. The photo I noticed the other night is sitting on the shelf. I squint my eyes.

Devon continues to speak. "After I realized that Norah was never coming back, I reached out to her sister, Naomi." He gestures to the photo across the room. "As you can see, the sisters are nearly identical, minus a few small differences. Which were easy to change."

He clears his throat. I look back at him. "It was actually Naomi's idea. She helped Norah and me launch Pepper. I explained to her about the experimental trial in Florida that might help Norah get better. And I told her that I needed money to pay off some debts on the restaurant."

He shakes his head. "We knew it was a long shot. I mean, I agreed she could probably pass as her sister. But we had to be careful. We were playing with fraud, and as a lawyer, I knew the consequences. She insisted it would work and told me she knew a chef named Luis who would help us. And so, we did it. We launched Thistle with Naomi as Norah Winthrop."

Devon runs a hand through his thick auburn hair and sits in his seat.

"Luis was actually a brilliant idea. He's a very talented chef and was able to work with all of Norah's existing recipes to recreate the magic we had at Pepper."

He stands up and begins to pace the room. He stops in front of a few awards on the bookshelf.

"But as I've told you before, the menu has started to become repetitive. And the reservation list was getting shorter. So I needed someone to step in. Someone like you."

I take a deep breath, trying to take in everything he's telling me. Of course, the explanation makes sense. But it just seems rather odd. I'm not a lawyer or a police officer, but I'm assuming there has to be something illegal going on here. He mentioned fraud.

If something illegal is going on here, *I can't be a part of it.*

"I'm sorry, Devon, for everything that's happened to you and your family." I lick my lips and breathe in deeply, trying to find the courage for what I have to say next.

I'm about to give up my dream.

"But I can't be a part of any of this. I don't want to be involved in anything illegal."

Devon walks over to me. He sits on the edge of his desk and grabs my hand in his. He looks at me the way someone looks at their new lover.

"Sadie, don't you see? We have a future together. We're a perfect match. You're talented, young. I have all the experience and the connections. I can make all your dreams come true." He begins to rub my hand, but I pull away.

"But this—it just feels wrong," I say, standing up from my

seat. "You lied to all those people about who Norah Winthrop was."

"But don't you see, Sadie? That's all in the past. We won't be doing anything illegal. All anyone will know is that Norah left, and you've been promoted."

He clasps his hands in front of his waist and leans back. "It's only a couple of years before I can get Norah into the trial. And then she'll get the help she needs, and we can focus on our future together."

I chew on my bottom lip. I can't deny it. The offer is tempting, but Devon has no idea who I really am or what I've done. He doesn't know about my time in prison. And what if there is something in this situation that might violate my probation? I shake my head, thinking of what that means.

"I'm sorry, Devon, I can't do this."

I get up and walk toward the door. Devon doesn't move, but as soon as I put my hand on the knob, he speaks up.

"Sadie, I didn't want it to come to this. But I don't think you have a choice."

I turn around and see that his expression has hardened. He crosses the room until he's a few feet in front of me. I feel my heart drop into my stomach.

"What do you mean I don't have a choice?"

"I know who you really are." He pauses. "Samantha Reynolds."

For the second time in forty-eight hours, my heartbeat shatters into a thousand beats. I feel my eyes widen and the color drain from my face. He takes another step toward me. I take a step back.

"I know all about your past. I know about the car accident and the Ohio Reformatory for Women. And that after you were released from prison, you legally changed your name so no one from your past could find you."

"Did you hire—"

But the truth is, I already know.

"Yes, I hired a private investigator to look around your past a little." He reaches out for my hand. I pull away.

"It was an accident. I was really young," I say, my voice quivering. "Believe me, it's not something I'll ever truly leave behind."

Devon leans in closer. "Listen, neither of us are perfect. Both of us have lied. This doesn't mean I don't care about you. In fact, I care about you more. More than I ever imagined I could care about anyone. Even Norah."

He reaches for me again. I take a step back toward the door, and he drops his hand.

"We have a future together, Sadie. Can't you see that? I promise that I'll always protect you. I'll make sure you never have to go to prison again."

I stare at him for a moment. My body is shaking like a leaf. Devon knows about my past. And he doesn't have to say what that means. It only takes one phone call to the police. He could claim that I've stolen something. Or that I didn't really have a place to live in the first place. Or worse, that I'm somehow involved in this fraud that he's created at Thistle.

And I realize in that moment that my dream may have just become my nightmare.

"Sadie, please. You can trust me."

I stare at him, my fear turning to anger.

"I guess I don't have a choice."

36

SADIE

I stand outside the back door to the kitchen at Thistle, my hand suspended over the door handle. Once I cross this line, there is no going back. Devon has already sent a message to all our reservations that there will be a new head chef on this evening's menu.

I take one last breath and turn the handle.

Once I'm standing in the threshold, I take in the whole scene. The staff are bustling around the kitchen, preparing a new menu. *My menu.*

The warm smell of the Wagyu being seared on the grill fills the room. Alex is whipping together the mousse I created in an industrial-size blender.

I close the door behind me.

Don't look back, I tell myself.

Because tonight I'm going to fulfill a dream I've had since I was a little girl. And if Devon gets me in so much trouble that I end up going back to jail? Then so be it.

At least I'll have this one dinner service.

I quickly get to work visiting each station and going over

preparations with the kitchen staff. I can't deny there's a buzz in the room that's contagious. Everyone seems genuinely excited to try out some new recipes. About an hour later, Devon walks into the room.

"Hey, everyone, can I have your attention?" he says. Everyone stops what they're doing and looks to the center of the room where he's standing. He gestures for me to join him. I walk over to stand with him, my heart racing once again.

"Tonight is our first night with the new menu created by our very own Sadie," he says. I feel myself blush slightly. "I want you all to put forth your very best work. One of the things I'm most proud of here at Thistle is how we work together as a team. So I'm excited to see what you all have in store for our guests tonight."

Devon reaches over and places a hand on my shoulder. I remain perfectly still. "And remember, there's a bonus for a flawless delivery tonight."

This causes a few smiles around the room. "Now get to work, team! Our first reservation is in three hours."

Everyone turns around and returns to their stations. There's a focused buzz around the room. Once all eyes have turned away, Devon turns to face me.

"Are we good, Sadie?" he says in a low voice.

"Yes," I say.

"Good," he replies. "You're going to do great, I promise. We'll celebrate later, okay?"

I nod, not trusting myself to respond. Devon leaves the kitchen.

For the next few hours, I push all thoughts of Norah and Devon to the back of my mind. All I focus on is what we have to accomplish tonight with the new menu. Ingrid pulls me aside to talk to the service team about what's on the menu.

As planned, we've pulled out all the stops for tonight's guests. When they arrive, Devon is offering them a complimentary glass of champagne. I have developed some sample appetizers that we call "amuse-bouche" that will be presented as soon as the guests are seated. Beef with cucumber parcels. Alex and I have worked together to create a variety of chocolate truffles nestled inside tiny gift boxes for guests to take home.

About halfway into the reservations, Devon walks back into the kitchen to find me.

"Sadie, I have someone I'd like you to meet," he says. "Come with me."

Just before we're about to walk into the dining room, he stops and turns to face me. He reaches up and tucks a few hairs behind my ears, then straightens my coat. When he raises his hand to pinch my cheeks, I flinch.

"I just want you to look your best, chef," he says. I glare at him.

When he's finished, he turns and walks into the dining room. I follow him to the corner of the room, where a table of men in suits are dining. Something about the way they look at me as we approach makes me feel uncomfortable.

"Sadie, this is Anthony, one of my close partners and investors in Thistle."

A man with cool gray eyes and a closely cropped beard smiles at me. He says nothing, but nods in my direction.

"Anthony, I'd like you to meet Sadie, our new chef."

"Hello," I say, giving a small wave. "How has everything been so far tonight?"

All of the men at the table look to Anthony.

"Everything has been fantastic, Sadie," he says. His tone is overly smooth, like a freshly greased wheel. "It looks like you have a bright future here at Thistle."

I'm not sure how to respond, but something about the way he talks makes me feel uncomfortable. He studies me while I struggle to find my words.

"Thanks," I finally manage. There's an awkward pause while Devon and I stand there. "Well, I'd better get back to the kitchen," I say. I turn on my heel and walk away before Devon can say anything else.

Devon stays at the table, and I overhear him say something like "Norah has moved on, but I think she's perfect, don't you?"

I guess it doesn't surprise me to hear him say that. But I also know that Norah—or whoever it is that looks exactly like Norah—has definitely not moved on.

The rest of the evening goes pretty flawlessly. I can't deny it, being in charge of the kitchen and seeing all of my ideas come to life is absolutely exhilarating. It's actually more thrilling than I even thought it would be. I've only been to one rock concert in my life, but I imagine this is what it must feel like to have the entire world at your feet.

Devon comes into the kitchen after our last reservation is complete. He carries with him a bottle of champagne and two glasses.

He picks up a fork and taps it against the side of the champagne glass.

"I have an announcement to make," he says. He pours a glass of champagne and holds it in his hand. "I'm happy to report that tonight's service was a success. I am so proud of each and every one of you for flawlessly executing Sadie's vision and bringing your own talent to the table. Not only will I be providing each of you with a bonus, but also a bottle of Dom Pérignon to share with your family."

The staff cheers. Devon pours me a glass and hands it to me.

"Now I'm going to raise my glass to Sadie," he says. "Congratulations, chef."

At that moment, everyone in the room starts clapping for me. I feel my face turn red hot. Once they're done clapping, everyone goes silent. They look at me expectantly.

"Thank you so much for everything you've done tonight." I tuck a strand of hair behind my ear. "You took a chance on a new menu, on me, and I am beyond grateful." I raise my glass. "So I thank all of you for making tonight a success."

There are more cheers and clapping around the room. For a moment, a brief moment, I'm floating on a cloud. It's a moment I never thought would actually happen. I mean, I always imagined what it would be like to run a highly esteemed kitchen. What it might feel like. But never at this point in my career. And I never knew it would feel this good.

I take a sip of my champagne and set it down on the table. Devon leans over and whispers in my ear. He's so close I catch a hint of his cologne.

"You're amazing."

It's in that moment I start to second-guess my anger from earlier. All the rationalizations start tumbling through my head. I mean, Devon is right—we both lied. He lied about Norah in the fire. I lied about my prison time and the accident.

Those things can be overlooked, right? Because I don't know if I can give up the way I feel right now. Like I'm on top of the world. Like I can do anything. It's like a drug.

And despite what happened with Norah, maybe it's time for me to look forward instead of looking back.

37

SADIE

The next two nights of service go pretty flawlessly. The lamb is cooked perfectly. The mousse receives rave reviews from the guests. Everyone from the kitchen staff to the service crew are all smiles. It's as if we infused the whole restaurant with a new burst of positive energy. I've been smiling so much my mouth is sore from it.

Devon keeps a professional distance from me. I assume he's giving me space to adjust to our new circumstances and enjoy my role as head chef. It's given me time to process everything that has happened to this point.

But after our final Saturday night service, he tells me to meet him in his office so we can talk.

I walk into his office and see him sitting behind his desk with his laptop open. He looks up when I walk in. There's a bottle of wine and two glasses sitting on his desk.

"Have a seat," he says. He reaches over and pours me a glass of wine. I hesitate for a moment, wondering if I can trust him. But a few seconds later I grasp the glass in my hand. As I let the cool liquid stream down my throat, I feel my whole body relax.

"Well, what do you think?"

"About the wine?"

He chuckles. "No, Sadie. About the last three days. Your first full shift as head chef. Is it everything you imagined?"

"Yes," I say a little breathlessly. "It's more than I imagined."

I could go on and on about the entire experience. It's been a dream. Truly the best three days of my life. But I hold my words, waiting for Devon to speak.

"I have a gift for you," he says. He pulls a red box from his desk drawer and sets it in front of me. We make eye contact.

"Go ahead, open it," he says. I pull off the satin ribbon and pry open the box. It's a pair of pearl earrings with small diamonds on top.

"They're beautiful," I say. "Thank you."

I don't think I've ever had a piece of jewelry this nice before. I run my thumb over the cool surface of the pearls.

"Listen, Sadie, I want to talk to you about the other night," he begins.

"Okay." I put the box down and pick up my wineglass.

"I know I came on a little strong." He tips his head to the side. "I shouldn't have brought up your prison history," he says. The look in his eyes seems earnest. "I just get a little stressed when I'm under a lot of pressure. I'm really sorry. I didn't mean for it to scare you." He takes a deep breath and lets it out. His chest falls. "If you want to leave, you can go."

I take a sip of wine. My eyes graze the lovely earrings.

I could go. I could get back in my car, drive back down the coast, find another job. I could start from scratch again. I mean, I've done it before, and I got this far.

But I can't deny the feeling that I felt this past weekend, the feeling of utter and pure joy. The feeling of being in the place I'm supposed to be. Running the kitchen. Creating menus.

If I'm being honest with myself, it's a drug I don't think I'm ready to give up.

"I understand," I say. "I'm sorry too. I shouldn't have lied to you. I was just so determined to get a job here. I thought if I got a chance to show you and Norah what I could do...it wouldn't matter what I did in the past."

Devon gives me a hopeful look. "So you'll stay?"

"Yes." I look him in the eyes. "I'll stay."

Devon's muscles relax. "I can't tell you how happy that makes me." He pulls some papers out of his desk. "I have the ingredients list for next week. Do you want to start planning the menu? Or take these back to the cabin with you?"

I bite my lip. This is a crazy situation, a situation I've never been in before. Not to mention the fact that I'm seventy-five percent certain I can't trust him.

But I can't deny it—I'm still attracted to Devon despite our encounter the other night.

"Why don't you come back to the cabin with me, instead?"

38

SADIE

Devon and I spend the next few days together, either working in the kitchen, going for walks around the garden, or traveling to meet with different local vendors. The week flies by, and before I realize it, it's already Thursday. I've brought a couple of new items to the menu, as well as some of the favorites from last week.

After the usual staff meeting, the kitchen staff get to work preparing for tonight's menu. Everyone falls into a rhythm. I'm silly with happiness as I walk around the room, making adjustments to each dish. The night is nearly half over, and we've had flawless service.

When I see Jessica approach with a half-eaten plate of food in her hand, my blissful state falters.

"Chef," she says, "one of the guests at table forty-four sent back this dish. He said it had way too much salt, and the sauce was cold."

I take a look at the dish. It's one of the preparations of lamb I created.

"Thanks, Jessica." I place the plate on the table. "I'll take care of this right away."

I make my way over to the station and work with the chef to have a hot dish created in just a few minutes. I decide to take the lamb out to apologize in person. Once I have the dish in hand, I smooth the front of my white chef's coat and twist one of my pearl earrings back into place. Pulling my shoulders back, I walk into the dining room directly to table forty-four.

As I step closer to the table, I realize it's the white-haired man Devon introduced me to the other night. He's with a young woman. My shoulders tense.

"Sir, I am so sorry about the lamb," I say, placing the plate down in front of him. "I hope this is more to your liking."

"Good evening, chef," he says in his overly smooth voice. "Do you remember me?"

"Yes. Anthony, correct?"

He nods and places an arm around the young woman. "You know, we have some high expectations for you here."

"Of course," I say as I feel a little heat rush to my cheeks.

"But this lamb?" he says. He picks up his steak knife and stabs the center of the lamb. I jump in spite of myself. The table shakes. A few of the other diners look over at us. "Norah would've never served us crap like this. In fact, this is the kind of food they serve in prison."

The last words sting. Now my cheeks are burning hot. I can't believe he just said that to me. Everyone else has loved the lamb. Is he taunting me on purpose? And why would he say *prison*? Unless Devon told him about me.

I'm so embarrassed at this point that my hands are trembling. I fumble with what to say and finally blurt out, "I'm sorry. I promise I'll do better next time."

"You'd better," he says in almost a whisper.

Before he can say anything else, I turn and walk briskly back to the kitchen. I spend a couple of minutes looking for Devon, but he's nowhere to be seen. So I continue working with the rest of the staff to finish the night's list of reservations. The rest of the evening goes fairly smoothly, but I'm rattled. I can't get the man's face out of my head.

At the end of the night, Devon walks into the kitchen right as we're cleaning up.

"Sadie, can you come to my office?"

"Of course," I say.

A few minutes later, the two of us are sitting across from each other at his desk. But this time there's no glass of wine waiting for me at the end of the shift. Not to mention the way he's looking at me right now makes me feel extremely uncomfortable. His body is so tense I can see the vein throbbing in his neck.

"Sadie, what happened tonight?"

Of course my thoughts immediately go to the customer at table forty-four.

"I don't know."

"What do you mean you don't know? Table forty-four. The lamb?"

It's as if the man who was in my bed last night is gone. His eyes have turned cold, vacant. He stares at me. The person I see across the table is someone I don't recognize.

I stare at him for a moment, trying to decide what to say next. What was I thinking? I mean, everybody makes mistakes, right? Nothing comes out perfect from the kitchen every night. Every kitchen has a margin of error. Devon is staring at me, waiting for my answer.

"I'm sorry, Devon. I made sure to bring him out a fresh rack of lamb right away."

"Sorry doesn't cut it, Sadie." He stands up from his desk and starts to pace the room. When he comes toward me, I actually flinch.

"Do you have any idea what is at stake here? I've put my entire career on the line for this restaurant. My time. My money." He points at his chest. "If I don't make this work, it's over for me."

He's standing over me now as I'm sat on the chair. My palms start to sweat.

"I'm sorry. Everybody makes mistakes," I say, my voice slightly shaky.

"Not at my restaurant. Honestly, Sadie, are you a complete idiot? Why would you send the lamb out cold?"

I feel a little bit of anger light up inside me. I get up out of the chair.

"You can't talk to me like that," I say. Our faces are now about six inches apart. My heart is beating so fast I think it might explode.

"I can talk to you however I want to talk to you, Sadie," he says and takes a step closer. "I own you."

I feel something inside me snap. When I was in prison, people tried to threaten me. Even beat me up. But I've never backed down from a bully.

"No you don't," I say, taking a step toward the door. "You said I can leave if I don't want to be here. So I'll leave."

"That's where you're wrong," he says, pointing his finger at my face. "It's been a while since we've taken inventory in the storeroom. It would be a shock if anything came up missing. Especially if those items showed up in your car later."

"Are you accusing me of stealing?"

He shrugs. "I wouldn't say that, but the police might think..."

I narrow my eyes at him.

"Go ahead. I'll take my chances with the police," I say, reaching for the door.

Devon grabs my arm roughly.

"You're not going anywhere," he growls. His face is inches from mine. I smell the alcohol on his breath.

"Let go of me!" I say, pulling my arm away. He tightens his grip.

"Where are you going to go next, Sadie? Are you going to find another restaurant where you can sleep your way to the chef's position?"

The anger inside me boils over. I rip my arm away from him, reach back, and slap him across the face. To my surprise, he slaps me in return. Pain explodes across my cheek.

Before I know what's happening, Devon grabs me by the neck and shoves me up against the door. He squeezes. Suddenly the room starts to blur. I slap my hands against his arm, trying to get him to release me.

I can't breathe. My chest burns. If he doesn't let go in a few seconds, I'm afraid I'm going to pass out. Then things start to go black. Suddenly he lets go. I slump to the floor.

"I thought we could work together, Sadie. Do this as a team. But you keep making the wrong choices," he says, standing over me. "So it looks like we're going to have to do this the hard way."

I sit there for a few seconds, holding my throat and

staring at the floor. My face is burning, my eyes stinging. I feel tears come to my eyes, but I try to hold my breath, refusing to cry in front of this man.

Devon hovers over me. When I finally stand up again, holding my hand to my face, he takes a step back.

"Go back to the cabin and think about what you did tonight," he says. "And don't even think about running away. Anthony, the man you botched the lamb for tonight? He's very well connected. In fact, not only does he know what prison you stayed at, but he also knows who you really are. So don't try to run. Because we'll find you."

I manage to make it to the doorway. I'm shaking like a leaf now. I rip open the door and run as fast as I can back to the cabin. Once Devon is out of sight, I let the tears flow. My face is burning, the tears running down my cheeks.

As I careen through the darkness, stumbling over the gravel pathway, I catch a light from the cabin at the back of the property. And I can't help but wonder...

Is this what it was really like to be Norah Winthrop?

39

SADIE

When I wake up on Sunday morning and move my body, it aches—most especially my face. Before I even go and look in the mirror, I gently touch the skin on my cheek. I can already tell it's swollen, which is horrible timing. Why? Because today I need to meet with Brian, my parole officer.

I was going to mention it to Devon last night, but obviously we didn't get to that. After the meeting, I felt utterly miserable.

I still can't believe what happened last night. Devon is like two different people, like Jekyll and Hyde. On the one hand, he's this successful restaurateur and caring lover. But on the other hand?

He's a monster.

A monster who now has complete control of my life.

When I was in prison, I would often hear stories of women who went on parole only to find themselves back behind bars just six months later. I swore when I left that would never be me. I would never do anything so stupid as to get put back in prison. But now I understand. Being an ex-con is full of nearly impossible decisions.

Once someone knows you've been in prison, they can hold that over you forever. It would only take one phone call to Brian or the police from Devon with the surveillance video he has of me.

The police would take one look at my record, and just like that, I'd be going back to jail.

When I finally do make it to the bathroom and look in the mirror, my left cheek is puffy and swollen. I gently apply a little bit of makeup and mascara and find some ice in the freezer to hopefully quell the swelling before I meet with Brian at Mike's Diner.

I send a text message to Devon and let him know that I have a meeting.

I have to meet with my parole officer Brian this morning.

A couple of seconds later a message pops up.

Where are you meeting?

Mike's Diner

A minute goes by. My stomach churns. What if he doesn't let me go? I mean, I'm sure he wants me to keep working here; wasn't that the point of threatening me last night?

Before my mind spins out all the possibilities, I get a message back.

Don't go far.

When I see the message, I feel a pit in my stomach.

I climb into my car a few minutes later and make my way out of the driveway of the Winthrop estate. One thought keeps tumbling through my mind.

I've left one prison behind, only to be locked up in another.

I PRACTICALLY JUMP when I hear the cling of the entry bell slapping the door as I walk into Mike's Diner. I managed to dig into the back of my trunk and find a hat. I pull it down as low as I can to cover my face. Not only do I want to avoid being recognized by any of my old customers, but I also want to hide the fact that I have a swollen cheek.

As I step into the diner, I quickly scan the room. Brian is in the back, already digging into his favorite sugar cream pie. I make my way in his direction. As I do, I catch Sally serving customers out of the corner of my eye. I avoid making eye contact with her.

I settle into the seat across from Brian. He puts down his fork and looks at me.

"Good morning, Sadie," he says.

"Good morning."

"So I hear you have a fancy new chef job. Congratulations."

"Yes," I say. "It's a dream come true." My voice sounds robotic. There's a fine line between dream and nightmare at this point.

"Everything is going well with the Winthrops? No issues?"

I look at Brian for a moment. I honestly debate whether I

should just tell him the whole story. About Naomi and Norah. About the fire. About Devon blackmailing me, then choking me.

But I stop myself. What good would it do? It's Devon's word against mine. And I'm a convict. No one will believe me, especially Brian.

"Everything is going fine," I say.

"I reached out to your boss, Devon Winthrop, for residence confirmation." He pauses. "I'm still waiting to hear back."

Just hearing Brian say his name out loud makes my skin crawl.

"I'll talk to him," I say, chewing on my lip. *Residence confirmation? From Devon?* No chance that's going to happen now.

"I needed it yesterday, Sadie," he says. He gives me a pointed look.

"I know, I know," I say. "I'll handle it."

"What happened to your face?" he asks, pointing his fork at my cheek. I subconsciously touch the side of my face.

"Oh, you know, I was running some dishes out to the dining room, and I ran into the wall." I make a weak attempt at a laugh. "It happens more than you think when you're running around the kitchen."

"Oh," he says. He tips his head to the side and squints his eyes. For a moment he acts like he might ask more questions. But just as he's about to speak, Sally shows up at our table.

"Good morning, you two," she says.

"Hey, Sally," I say. I hope that because of my hat and the angle from where Sally is standing, she can't see the swelling and bruising on my face.

"Sadie, what happened to your face?"

I feel my cheeks burn. *Too late.* I make direct eye contact with Sally.

"Oh, you know me, clumsy as ever, right?"

It only takes her a split second to catch on. "Good lord, child. I've never met anyone as graceless as you. There are still stains on the ceiling from when you tripped and threw the jug of mayonnaise into the air."

I look at Brian and shrug. He rolls his eyes.

"All right then, you guys, let me know if you need anything. I'll be around," she says, giving me a little wink.

Brian takes the last bite of his sugar cream pie and then pushes the plate away.

"Well," he says, "I think I have everything I need here, Sadie. Unless there's something you want to tell me..." He pauses for a moment, looking me in the eye.

I stay completely still. I realize this is my last chance to tell him about what's going on at Thistle. But I just don't see how that scenario could ever work out in my favor. So I simply shrug my shoulders and give him a thin smile.

"No, everything's great."

"Okay then." Brian gets up from the table. "I'll see you next month."

He throws down a five-dollar bill on the table to cover the pie and the coffee, then heads toward the door. I sit in the booth for a few more minutes to make sure that he's left before I get up to leave.

As I'm walking out the door, Sally comes up next to me.

"That mark on your face? I don't think you ran into a door, kiddo."

I forget sometimes that not only does Sally know who I truly am, but she's also been through some troubling times of her own. Either way, I can't tell her what's going on. The last thing I need is to get someone else involved in this mess that I've made of my life.

"Sally, it's fine."

I can tell Sally is not convinced, but she shrugs. "Well, I heard you got a new job and you're head chef now at Thistle. I'm proud of you, kid," she says.

She gives me a playful elbow. "You know you can call me if you ever need anything, right?"

"Right, I know. Thanks. I have to go," I say.

Sally turns and heads back to her customers, who are all calling for more coffee and more eggs.

I walk out the front door into the parking lot. As I do, I look over and catch sight of an older man walking toward the front door of Mike's Diner. The way he holds his shoulders, the slight limp—he looks really familiar.

And then it hits me.

It's Charlie, the pastry chef from Thistle. Even though I'm trying to avoid anyone seeing me in my current state, I call out his name.

"Charlie! Is that you?"

Charlie looks up, and I see that it really is him. He walks a few steps toward me, and we meet in the middle of the parking lot.

He's wearing a sweatshirt and jeans. I realize I've never even seen him in his street clothes before, only in the white chef's uniform.

"Hi, Sadie," he says. "How's it going over there at Thistle?"

"It's going well, actually. I've been promoted. I was actually able to create my own menu, which Thistle has been serving for the last two weekends."

"Wow, Sadie, that's amazing!" His smile is genuine.

"Thanks," I say. For a moment, I've forgotten about the rest of it. "So why did you leave Thistle?"

"Leave?"

"Well, Devon told me that you quit. Something about not wanting to work with Norah anymore?"

A strange look crosses Charlie's face. He squints his eyes at me in confusion.

"Sadie, I didn't quit Thistle. I was fired."

The revelation takes my breath away. "What? But Devon told me you quit."

Charlie shakes his head. "No, I didn't quit. Norah fired me. She said my work wasn't good enough to work in the kitchen at Thistle anymore." He shakes his head. "I guess I just thought you were my replacement."

"Oh, Charlie, I'm so sorry," I say. Although after everything I've learned the last few weeks, I think it was probably a blessing in disguise.

"No, I'm old. I'll be fine," he says. He gives me a pat on the arm. "It was good to see you, Sadie. Good luck."

"Thanks, you too."

Charlie continues into the diner. I make my way to the car. As I turn on the ignition and pull back onto the highway, I think about what Charlie told me.

It doesn't make any sense. Why would Naomi fire Charlie? Unless her intention was to have me replace him as pastry chef. Is it possible that Naomi was helping me? I chew on this idea a little bit longer. And I start to think about everything that's happened up to this point.

When I start to put the pieces together, it all starts to make sense. Naomi is the one who hired me. Naomi is the one who promoted me. She's the one who fired Charlie. Once he was gone, Naomi made her exit.

And now she's gone. And I'm here.

I don't go directly back to Thistle. I simply drive around for an hour, thinking about everything. And by the time I pull back into the driveway of the Winthrop estate, I think I might have a plan to get myself out of this mess.

40

SADIE

When Monday comes, I find myself back at work. The kitchen is mostly empty at the beginning of the week, leaving me to work alone. The bruise on my face is still a pale shade of purple. I've mostly covered it up with makeup, but if someone were to look closely, they'd know what it was.

Every time the back door to the kitchen opens, I practically jump out of my skin. I've spilled my coffee twice this morning when someone knocked at the door. At any moment, Devon could walk in. I have no idea what kind of mood he's in.

Ingrid walks up to me while I'm going over the menu for the week.

"Good morning, chef," she says in her tight voice. "Is there anything you need help with today?"

I hold my breath, waiting for her to ask about my face, but she says nothing.

"No, I don't think so," I say. "Have you seen Devon?"

Ingrid shakes her head. "No, he informed me this

morning he was leaving for the city. He'll be gone until tomorrow evening."

I feel a flutter in my stomach. This is what I've been waiting for. An opportunity when Devon is gone so I can maybe sneak into his office. Alone.

"Okay, thank you, Ingrid," I say.

I decide to wait until it's dark to break into his office. In the meantime, I make some notes on the menu. In order for my plan to work, I need this week's service to be tweaked a bit. I don't want to make any changes big enough to alarm the staff, but my intention is to serve a less than stellar menu.

I bite the end of my pencil. It's more than that. I want to sabotage the entire weekend. I need Devon to find me completely incompetent for this to work.

I manage to keep myself busy until about six o'clock. Ingrid has left for the day, and we are now closed for deliveries. I pull on my jacket and zip it closed. The temperature has dropped dramatically over the last couple of weeks. The first snow in Maine usually happens around mid-November, but it feels like it may come much earlier this year.

As I step out into the darkness, a cold shiver runs up my spine. I'm not sure if it's the thinner air or my nerves. The light from Norah's cabin glows from across the lake. I tuck in my bottom lip, thinking about everything I've learned up to this point.

It was hard for me to believe what Devon told me about the fire. That it was an accident. That they found Norah already burned. In fact, there's a small part of me that believes maybe Devon had something to do with starting the fire. After the way he's treated me over the last few weeks, I wouldn't put it past him.

And the way Naomi made her exit right after I stepped

up as pastry chef—it was as if she was grooming me to take over for her. It was cruel, really. She knew what Devon and his investors were like. She practically fed me to the wolves.

But tonight, I hope to turn the tables in my favor. If I can find something, anything, in Devon's office to tie him to the lies he's been telling about Norah's identity, I'll have the leverage I need to get out.

I weave my way through the property, careful to avoid the security cameras. After Devon revealed his true nature to me, I took a long walk and found out where all the cameras are placed on the property. The last thing I need is for him to have any more leverage over me.

When I arrive at Devon's office door, I'm pretty certain that I've successfully avoided every camera I could find.

Now the real challenge begins. How do I get into his locked office?

I thought about this quite a bit when I was driving home from the diner. The best solution I could come up with was picking the lock on the door. I figured the simple bobby-pin trick you see on TV wouldn't cut it. The internet is patchy out here, but I managed to get enough of a signal to find some solutions courtesy of YouTube, of which there were many. After about an hour of watching videos, I knew just what I needed. So on my way back to the farm, I stopped off at a hardware store, where a kind old man helped me find a hook and pick set.

I stayed up late practicing, but as I stare down at the door, my palms begin to sweat. I'm not really sure if I can do this. I take a deep breath and exhale.

After what feels like an eternity of jiggling the locks and failing, they finally click into place. The door to Devon's office swings open.

It's completely dark inside. I'm greeted by the familiar smell of whiskey and sandalwood, which sends a shiver down my spine. It's like he's here still, his scent hanging in the air. I close the door quietly behind me, shake off my nerves, and head to his desk.

What I'm looking for is any type of paperwork that might help me understand what happened. I pry open the bottom drawer of his desk, which is full of file folders. I pull them out and place them on his desk. I use the light from my phone to scan the pages. Most of it is legal filing, mixed in with some paid invoices and letters from the bank. All of it is related to Thistle. After about thirty minutes of going through all the papers, I come up with exactly nothing.

I put all the papers back exactly as I found them. I go through a few more drawers with the same result. I sit back in the leather desk chair.

Now what?

I pull up my phone to check the time, and as I do, the light from my phone catches on something across the room. The photo of Norah, Naomi, and Devon.

I walk over to the photo and attempt to pull it from the shelf. It seems to be stuck. I pull again, and I hear a click. The sound makes me jump.

A portion of the bookcase swings open. I pull it open wider and catch my breath.

It's Devon's safe. I remember Luis saying something about how he keeps too much cash on hand. This must be where he stashes it.

My shoulders slump. I may have managed to pick the door lock, but there's no way I'm cracking this safe. I shine my light around the edges of the safe, just in case there's something else he might have stashed in here.

There's a small gap between the trim and the top of the safe. I run my hand alongside it. That's when I feel an envelope. I pull it out.

The envelope feels heavy in my hands. I walk over to the desk and empty the contents onto the top. There are a couple of folders. I open the paperwork and see that it is medical records. I start reading through. The medical records are from the fire. In fact, they're hospital records detailing Norah's injuries. As I read through, it states that Norah is completely incapacitated from the fire.

Underneath this stack is another set of papers that are nearly identical.

But when I look at the names and the social security number, they've been changed. The name and the injuries of this record are listed under Naomi.

I bite my lip. So that's how he did it; he fudged records so that if anyone asked questions about the woman in the back cabin, he could provide evidence that it was Naomi.

And now I have evidence that they both committed fraud.

I eagerly flip through the rest of the pages, my heart pounding. My fingers pull out a letter from Hammond Insurance. The first line surprises me the most.

We are pleased to inform you that your claim for fire damage has been processed. Please find the attached enclosed check for $800,000.

I stare at the page. *So he did get the insurance money. But where did it go?*

I hear an owl hooting outside, nearly causing me to jump. I know Devon is gone, but I need to get out of here.

There are a couple of pages left in the folder. I quickly scan them and realize they are police reports. Just like the medical records, there are two sets. One with Norah listed as the injured party, and one with Naomi. Not to mention, the last document removes any reference to arson.

I quickly stuff the pages back in the folder, tuck it into my jacket, and make my way toward the door. I manage to lock it quietly behind me. The cold air bites my cheeks as I step into the darkness, but I hardly notice.

All I can think about is how I'm going to use these papers under my jacket to free myself from this prison.

41

SADIE

Devon returns on Thursday evening, about an hour before our first reservation. I'm in the middle of reviewing the menu with the staff when he walks in.

The room goes silent. He makes eye contact with me, and with a few strides, we are standing side by side at the head of the table.

"Hello, everyone," he says. He steps up next to me and places a hand on my back. I stand perfectly still, even though I want to smack his hand away. "Sorry I'm late; traffic from New York was thick." He clears his throat. "I trust Chef Sadie has done a good job of prepping for tonight's service, but if you need anything, I'll be in my office."

He gives a curt nod and turns on his heel. When he leaves the room, my body sags with relief. His absence from the kitchen will make this so much easier.

The reservations begin at six. We have a full roster of guests, and the food goes out like clockwork. I personally inspect each dish before it goes to the table. I make some *changes.*

I add a teaspoon of salt to the mousse, destroying the flavor profile. I drizzle the lamb with a little chocolate sauce, masking the perfect seasoning that's already on the meat. I make the tweaks subtle, under the guise of creating a "unique" flavor. But I know exactly what I'm doing.

By seven o'clock, the entire kitchen is in chaos. Nearly every single plate comes back to the kitchen barely touched. There are numerous complaints from customers. I let up on my changes at the end, just so we can finish the service.

Devon storms into the kitchen at eight. His face is red, jaw clenched.

"Good evening, everyone. I just got off the phone with the fire department. We have a gas line leaking near the property. For the safety of our staff and guests, we are closing the kitchen for the rest of the night. Please clean your station and go home for the night."

"Sadie," he says, gritting his teeth, "please see me in my office."

I thought he was going to hit me right then and there in front of the staff, but he doesn't. He balls up his fists and storms out of the room.

So far my plan is going well.

When I arrive outside his office, I hesitate and lightly touch my face, which is mostly healed from the other night. My hand shakes as I reach out and knock on the door. Whatever happens next, I know it's for the best. If he beats me, it's a necessary evil.

Or else I'll never get out of this place.

"Come in," I hear him say from the other side of the door.

I barely set a foot in the room before he starts berating me.

"Sadie, what the heck were you thinking tonight? This is a disaster. Do you know how much money it's going to cost me to keep this quiet?"

"Devon, I'm sorry. I was just trying to make each dish unique. The best chefs take risks, so I thought—"

"Unique? A couple of customers called your lamb with chocolate sauce downright disgusting." He points a finger at me. "You'd better pull your head out of your ass, Sadie, or I'm going to make it extremely difficult for you."

"Tomorrow night will be better, I promise," I say.

Devon shakes his head. "We're closing for the rest of the weekend."

Now I'm confused.

"Why?"

Devon exhales. "Haven't you heard your staff talking about it? There's a massive snowstorm coming. Beginning tonight. We don't want anyone driving out here and getting stranded. Or worse."

I stare at him for a moment, processing the news. *I may need to rethink my plan.*

"Now, please get out of my sight."

I quickly slip out the door before he can change his mind. My body sags with relief. He didn't physically touch me, which I consider a win.

I head to my room and set my alarm for two a.m. I stare at the ceiling for a few minutes, willing my heartbeat to slow down enough to fall asleep. But before I know it, exhaustion takes over, and I'm drifting off.

The alarm startles me when it goes off. I sit straight up in my bed. I'm already dressed, so I pull off the covers and walk to the window. Peeling back the curtain, I breathe a sigh of relief. Just as I expected, there are only a few lights on around the property. All I have to do is slip on a pair of boots and make my way to the kitchen.

I make sure to stay in the shadows as I weave my way around the property. It's eerily quiet outside, the only sound a few birds cooing in the distance. When I arrive at the back door to the kitchen, I take one last look around, take a deep breath, and then slip inside the door.

Using my phone as a flashlight, I step into the room, my heartbeat pounding in my ears. The quicker I find what I need, the less chance I have of being caught.

42

NAOMI

I stare in the rearview mirror. The skyline of New York is fading behind us. It represents so much more than just a city. It represents a past. A past that I can't wait to put behind me.

Luis and I are headed south. Specifically, Palm Beach, Florida. Luis has some connections and has potentially found a position as a chef at a local restaurant. I was relieved that he didn't even suggest I come to work with him.

Like I said, I have no desire to see the inside of a restaurant kitchen ever again.

As for me? I've accepted a position at a pharmaceutical company called Triad. The same pharmaceutical company that offers the trial medication for brain injury recovery.

So I did some research. I found a thread on Reddit where someone had gotten a position at a pharmaceutical company and they were able to work themselves up the chain. Once they got into a management position, they were able to pull some strings and get a family member a coveted spot on a medical trial. It seems like a long shot, but it might be the only way Norah will ever be able to get help.

So we're going to start a new life near the beach. And the only thing I can bank on is that Devon will continue to care for my sister until I can afford to bring her down to stay with us.

Sometimes I wonder if Norah even knows what's going on. It's been a couple of years since she's had a scan for brain activity, and I could swear there's been a couple of times when she blinked and maybe even recognized me. I know I don't have forever to get her the help she needs.

I used all the money I made from working at Thistle to pay off my portion of the debt to Devon's investors. The only consolation I have is the cell phone that I left for my sister. I tucked it underneath the recliner she sits in every day. I told the nurse that if anything ever happens or she sees any sign of a struggle, then she is to text me immediately. I programmed my number into the phone.

I'm going to be checking in with the nurse weekly to make sure everything's okay. I try to relax my shoulders. That's all I can do for now.

Luis reaches over and squeezes my hand. "You ready to pull off the road and get something to eat?"

I squeeze back. "Sure," I say. "Something greasy sounds good."

Luis smiles and rolls his eyes. I can't wait for a cheeseburger. And to gain a little weight again, to feel like I'm back in my own body. Norah might have valued that tiny waist, but I'm done with it.

We find a booth in the corner of the diner, and I leave Luis there while I run to the restroom. As I'm walking into the bathroom, I feel my phone buzz. I don't have a ton of contacts on my phone, so I'm surprised that someone would be messaging me.

I just hope it isn't Devon.

I go to the restroom, wash my hands, and just as I'm about to leave, I pull out my phone. When I look down, I see a text message from an unknown number. I swipe open my phone and gape at the message. It contains images of some paperwork. I scan the words and realize what they are. Medical records, police reports. The last page is from Hammond Insurance. When I read the letter, it feels like someone has wrapped their hands around my heart and squeezed.

How could he?

Tears push their way up to my eyes. Then I see the text bubble start moving, signaling a message.

> If you don't want me to take this to the police, you'll come back.

My heart sinks into my stomach. The message isn't signed, but I know who sent it.

Sadie.

That little brat. She must have broken into Devon's office.

I stare at the message. If she has the documents, I'm screwed. The police will come after me.

I message back.

> What do you want?

A few seconds later, there's a response.

> I need your help. Then we can both be free.

I bite my lip. I look across the room at Luis, who's drinking his soda. We were so close.

I'll be there tonight.

I cross the room and sit down at the table. Luis immediately knows something is wrong. He's ordered us a couple of burgers. Even though I've been looking forward to the burger for the last ten miles, I've suddenly lost my appetite.

He puts down his burger.

"Tell me," he says.

"It's Sadie. She found out about the swap." I lick my lips. "She has proof."

Luis leans forward. "So what do we do now?"

"I have to go back. She wants my help."

He furrows his brow. "To do what?"

"My guess? Take down Devon."

Luis swirls the straw in his glass. "What about the storm?"

My heart stops. "What storm?"

"There's a storm coming in from Canada. It's supposed to be a really bad one. They're predicting over a foot of snow. I heard one of the truckers mention it when he came in."

That's not good.

"I have to try."

"I'll go with you," he says.

"No." I shake my head. "You've done enough, Luis. Go back to Florida. Find a job; forget about this whole mess."

"We're in this together." Luis reaches across the table and grabs my hand. "Until the end."

A lump forms in my throat. I nod. The truth is, I need his

help. But it's so much to ask. Before I can say another word of protest, Luis gets up from the table.

"How about we get these burgers to go."

43

SADIE

I wake up at noon on Friday. It's the first time I've actually slept through the night in three months. I crawl out of bed and look out the window. Devon was right. There's already at least six inches of snow that's fallen overnight.

I also hear a large mechanical humming sound coming from the restaurant. At first, I think maybe a snowplow has come. I pull on some jeans and a pair of boots and go to the front door. But I'm only able to get it open about three inches when I push it.

I walk back to the window, open it and stick my head out. I realize that the sound is coming from the generator that Devon has set up on the property. Which means the power must be out. I remember him saying something about a generator that will power the bare minimum until the storm passes.

I walk into the living room, where there's a large gas fireplace. I flip the switch to turn it on. It takes a few minutes, but then a small flame leaps to life. In the kitchen, I open up the refrigerator and grab a basket of eggs. I use the gas stove to make an omelet and brew some coffee. As I do, I think about what happened last night.

I used the cover of darkness to sneak into the kitchen. There is a binder for food orders we keep on a table near the hallway. I was afraid Devon might catch me snooping through past orders if I looked during the day, so this felt like the safest route. I leafed through past purchase orders from our vendors. I was looking for something very specific, *a phone number*.

Most of the orders went through Thistle, listing the restaurant's main phone line as the preferred contact number. But I had a hunch that maybe the number I was looking for might be listed as well.

After about twenty minutes of searching, I found what I needed. There, listed as a backup contact for an order of cremini mushrooms, was Naomi's cell phone number.

I programmed her number into my phone and tucked the purchase order back into its place. My heart was pounding so loud in my ears I was sure Devon could hear me from across the property. I tiptoed through the kitchen to the back door and stepped outside. The snow was just beginning to fall. I backtracked in the dark and slipped into the cabin, avoiding any cameras so he wouldn't catch me.

At least, I hoped he hadn't spotted me.

It took me about an hour before my heartbeat settled back to normal after I'd climbed into bed, but I must have fallen asleep.

Now here I am. The smell of burnt eggs wafts up to my nose. I must have gotten lost in my thoughts, burning my omelet. I pull it off the oven and slide it onto a plate.

Now I wait. Of course, I feel extremely anxious because there is a chance that Devon may just show up at my door today and beat the crap out of me. But I don't think he'll do that. I think he needs time to figure out what he's going to do now that I've shown him I'm not as capable as he thought I was.

I sip my coffee at the small dining table and watch the snow continue to fall outside.

My thoughts drift back to my father. I wish he were here to help me. But at least I made his dream come true. It's just, the dream didn't turn out exactly the way I had planned. If I do make it out of this situation alive, I might need to rethink my career path. Maybe this work isn't for me.

Hours pass and still no visit from Devon. It's a relief in some ways, but as day turns into night, an uneasy feeling builds in my gut. The sky continues to dump loads of snow on the ground. The generator continues to hum outside, but there's no sign of a snowplow. It's just me, Devon, and Norah on the property.

If he decides to come over to the cabin, I'm pretty much a sitting duck.

At about nine o'clock that night, I decide to open a bottle of red wine to calm my nerves. I alternate between sitting by the fire and pacing around the room.

When I hear a knock on my door, I almost leap across the room. Then I notice how quiet it's become. The generator power seems to have weakened. The cabin has gone dark except for the light flickering from the fireplace.

I put my glass of wine down on the table and make my way to the door. My hands tremble as I slowly reach for the knob.

I open the door. The person standing in front of me is not Devon.

"Hello, Sadie," says Naomi.

I step aside and let her into the room.

44

NAOMI

"How did you find the papers?" I ask.

The two of us are sitting at the table in the cabin, the light from the fireplace casting long shadows into the room. Sadie has drawn the curtains so that we can have some privacy.

I know it's only a matter of time before Devon figures out I'm here. But at least we have a few minutes. I came straight to see Sadie after checking on my sister.

After Luis and I left the diner, we jumped in his truck and drove straight through the night to get here. It took about six hours. Luckily for us, most of the roads were still open.

But now? The roads are most certainly closed.

Luis stopped and checked us in at a hotel down the highway. I made sure the front desk attendant saw my face before we made our way to the room. Then we took the back stairwell and slipped out into the parking lot.

There's a back entrance to the Winthrop property that the nurse uses to come and go without being seen by the staff. Luis turned off the truck lights, and I used the access road to make my way to Norah's cabin. I did the best I could to make sure Devon wasn't there before I walked inside, relieved to find that Norah was completely fine.

Then I made my way over to Sadie's cabin. And now she's glaring at me in the dimly lit room. It's dark, but I'm pretty sure her face is red with rage.

"The safe," she says.

"You broke in?"

She shakes her head. "No, it was tucked above the safe, in between the trim. Whatever he's keeping in that safe, it must be full."

My stomach twists. I figured Devon had an insurance policy, but I never imagined he kept paperwork from the fire. I suddenly notice the bruises on her arm and a fading bruise on her left cheek and feel guilty.

"Sadie, I'm sorry," I say.

"You're sorry, Naomi? I mean, that's your name, right?"

I say nothing but give a small nod.

"Sorry doesn't even begin to cut it." She starts pacing the room. "You brought me here. You fired Charlie so I could move up in the kitchen. And you practically handed me over to your evil, sadistic brother-in-law slash husband or whatever he is."

I bite the corner of my mouth. I mean, technically she's right about all of that. But I didn't really have a choice. I remind myself that she's not totally innocent either.

"Let's be honest, Sadie, you did a lot of the heavy lifting yourself. All I did was provide you with the opportunity. You're the one who lied on your résumé. You're the one who decided to sleep with Devon. And you were the one who was desperate enough to work here even after you found out how things are run."

Sadie sits back in her seat. She looks gaunt. In just the few days I've been gone, she looks like she's lost ten pounds. There are dark circles under her eyes. I can tell this whole situation has taken a toll on her.

"But I am sorry." I glance away. "I just...I just didn't think it would go this far."

Sadie glowers at me from across the table. I'm not sure what she's going to say. She could hand me over to Devon, and then we would both be stuck here.

"I've heard Devon's side of the story," she says. "But why don't you tell me what really happened between the three of you."

So I walk her through the last three years. How we started Pepper together. How I left. The fire. The plan that Devon hatched up to pay back the investors. The meeting.

"He said that was your idea," she says.

I let out a puff of air. "My idea? No way. Devon didn't give me a choice. And once he found out that Luis was a talented chef? Knowing that he was my boyfriend? He pretty much told us that if we didn't do what he said, he was going to turn us over to the guys who loaned him the money. Not only that, if Luis didn't go along with it, he'd find a way to get his green card application delayed, indefinitely."

I let all of that sink in with Sadie. Hopefully she starts to see the whole picture.

"And the medical trial? The one that Devon promised me he would get my sister into to help her get better? He never had any intention of doing that. I knew the only way I could get out of this mess and help my sister was if I left."

I smooth the hair from my eyes. "And the only way I could leave is if he found a replacement."

"Me," she says.

I shrug. She has all the cards in her hands now. The room is silent for a few minutes save for the hum of the generator outside. Sadie takes another sip of her wine.

"While you were gone, I came up with an idea," she says finally.

"I'm all ears."

Sadie spreads her palms on the table. "The safe. I overheard Luis talking to Devon one night about the money in his safe. That Devon keeps a ton of cash in there."

"It's true," I say, nodding. "He keeps a few hundred thousand dollars cash in there. I walked in one time and found him standing in front of it with the door open. He told me it's our insurance policy against Anthony."

"The safe opens with a fingerprint," she says.

I narrow my eyes. *I can see where this is going.*

"It won't work."

"Why?"

"If we steal that money and flee, he'll come after us," I say. What I don't say? Anthony's men will be after us too.

"Don't you remember? I have proof he committed fraud."

I raise my eyebrows. "Wouldn't that implicate me too?"

Sadie shakes her head. "You were forced to go along with it. You could just tell the police how he physically threatened you. How he threatened your sister." She glances at my arm. "I'm sure the staff could testify that you had a lot of bruises over the years."

I rake my teeth over my bottom lip, considering this. Sadie continues.

"But from what you've told me, you could give the police

something better. You could give them Anthony Bello. That's *your* insurance policy."

I sit back in my chair. She's right. I'm sure the police would be happy to arrest Anthony for fraud. Not to mention the money they've been pulling in from the restaurant, which I presume they're laundering through the storage facility.

I swallow. I was trying to get *away* from those guys though, not piss them off more.

"I'm not sure that's the best decision for my own safety," I say. Sadie waves a dismissive hand.

"It won't come to that. Devon doesn't want to go to jail. Trust me, he's not going to call your bluff."

"I'm not sure..."

I put my elbows up on the table and rub my forehead, trying to find any fault in her plan. I have to admit, she has surprised me. The girl is a survivor.

"Think of what you could do with the money. Think of Norah."

I look over at her. The thing is, she's right.

"Okay," I say.

"Okay?"

"I'll do it."

"Great," she says. "Now here's what I was thinking..."

We spend the next couple of hours going over a plan in more detail. And for the first time, I feel like this could actually work. I message Luis, who's waiting back at the hotel. We're going to need his help.

Sadie picks up her phone and takes a seat next to me. The two of us huddle together as she types out a message to Devon.

Can you meet me in the kitchen? I'm really sorry about what happened last night, and I want to make it up to you

The two of us hold our breath. A few minutes later, I see the bubbles pop up on her phone.

He types back.

See you in 30 minutes

45

SADIE

"Sadie, I'm glad you finally came around," Devon says as he walks through the back door of the kitchen. He's wearing a pair of snow boots and a large parka, which he pulls off, sending snow flying all over the back of the room.

I'm sitting on a small stool at one of the chef's stations. While I waited for him, I put together a small charcuterie board with caviar, aged cheeses, figs, and a small loaf of bread. I arranged it on the table, alongside a bottle of wine and two glasses.

"I just feel terrible for how I messed things up," I say. Devon makes his way across the room, stopping at my table and picking up a glass of wine. I've pulled out two stools for us to sit down. He takes the one across from me.

Even though the generator puts off some heat, it doesn't bring the heat back to full power. Despite the chilly temperature in the room, I am sweating profusely. The long-sleeved sweater I'm wearing clings to my skin. I try my best not to let Devon see how nervous I am.

"I know it's a lot of pressure working in a new restaurant," he says.

I nod. "I guess I wasn't as ready as I thought I was," I say. "I hope we can work things out."

He smiles and reaches over to touch my hand.

He's taking the bait. I have about ten minutes to keep him busy until Naomi gets back. And so I play right into his hands.

It's sort of disgusting, really. This is the same person who smacked me across the face a week ago. Now he's acting like nothing happened and playing my mentor. Devon reaches over and grabs my other hand.

"I hope so too, Sadie," he says. I resist the urge to flinch at his touch.

I have to keep this going.

"I've been under a lot of pressure as well. I just feel terrible that I lashed out at you. I hope you can forgive me. I promise it won't happen again." He rubs his thumb across my hand. "I still believe we have a bright future together."

He releases my hand for a moment, reaching for his glass of wine.

"In fact," he says after he takes a sip, "I was speaking with some of my investors, and we're actually looking at opening the cabins in the spring. It'll bring in more customers, and we can serve dinner six nights a week."

The thought makes my stomach turn. I can't imagine working with him six days a week. I play along, picking up my own glass.

"With your talent and my vision?" he continues. "We can turn this place into a multimillion-dollar business."

It's funny how a few weeks ago I would've bought all of

his bullshit. I would've seen the future too. But now? I see it all so differently.

I pull up my glass for a toast. "To the future," I say.

Devon clinks my glass and finishes the wine. I pull the glass to my lips, then set it on the table.

There's a sound at the back of the room. Naomi walks in. Devon nearly jumps out of his seat. "What the hell are you doing here?"

"I told you I would be back for my sister, remember?" says Naomi.

He puts down the glass and stands. His back is facing me.

"I thought you never wanted to see this place again," Devon says. "That's what you told me when you left."

"You're right. I did say that," she says. "But I got a message from a friend."

She nods in my direction. Devon spins on his heel. I back up a few steps to put some distance between us. Naomi is standing in the doorway. I step over to the side of the table and grab one of the knives, just in case.

"I've always wondered what my sister would tell me if she got her memory back, Devon."

Devon starts to walk toward her. He stumbles. "Nothing you don't already know."

"Maybe. Or maybe she'd tell me who really started the fire."

"I've told you a million times, Naomi. It wasn't me."

"You're lying." Her voice is shaking as she speaks, and she's trembling. "Just like you lied to me about the insurance money. I know about the check, Devon. Sadie told me."

He glances over at me. I've made my way around the kitchen to stand next to Naomi.

"How did you know—"

"I found the paperwork you hid above the safe. The police reports, the medical records." The color drains from his face. "It's pretty straightforward fraud, Devon. Enough to send you to prison."

"You wouldn't do it," he says.

Devon tries to take a step toward me and stumbles. He reaches over to the table to steady himself while I point the knife toward Devon. He looks at me.

"Stay put," I say. My voice is shaking.

"Or what? You'll stab me with a knife?" His words are starting to slur. His expression changes. "I'm not feeling so good," he says.

His eyes go wide as he looks at me. "Sadie, what did you do?"

"Just a little extra spice in your wine," I say.

"You little—"

He lunges toward me but trips and falls sideways before he can reach me. As his body falls to the floor, his head slams into the side of the counter.

Naomi and I stay frozen for a moment. After a minute or so, we creep over to him. His eyes are closed.

"Is he breathing?" I ask.

Naomi kneels down and places her hand on his chest. It rises and falls. "Yes, he's just unconscious."

There's a two-inch gash on his head that's dripping blood onto the floor.

"His head," I say, pointing at the cut. "Should we clean it up?"

Before she can answer, the lights flicker in the room. "What was that?" I say.

She looks up. "The generator, it must be running out of gas. Quick, pick him up, and let's move him to his office."

Naomi grabs him under the arms. I grab his feet. He's heavier than he looks. We make our way to the back door. As we step into the snow, the cold bites at my cheeks. Devon has cleared a path from his office to the kitchen, which helps, but it's still difficult to carry him through the snow.

"And you're sure the cameras are out?" I ask as we push through the darkness.

"Yes," Naomi says. "They don't run on the generator power. We're almost there."

The door is unlocked. With some effort, we push him in and prop him up on his office chair. Then we roll it over to the bookcase. Naomi picks up the frame and pulls on the lever. It swings open.

I use Devon's finger to open the safe. It pops open easily, and I stare at the contents.

"Wow, that's a lot of cash," I say. There's an overhead light in the room. It flickers.

Naomi hands me a backpack. "We'd better hurry."

The two of us fill the backpacks until the safe is empty. Naomi closes the safe door and replaces the frame just as Devon begins to stir in his chair.

"We need to keep him locked up somewhere until we're gone," she says. "Otherwise, he'll try to follow."

"Where?"

"The freezer has a lock on it," she says.

"Isn't that too cold?"

She shakes her head. "The temperature rises to 40 degrees while the generator is on, to conserve power. It won't be too cold."

"Okay," I say. We pick him up again and head back out into the cold. He moves a couple of times, but to my relief, we make it back into the kitchen. I step over the pool of blood from his fall, and we carry him to the walk-in freezer.

Inside, we drop him on the floor and close the door. Naomi pulls the keys out of his pocket as we step out. She closes the door and locks it.

"That should hold him," she says. Her eyes dart over to the table where I had set up the charcuterie board. "Your wineglass," she says. "Wash it and put it back."

I do as she says, taking it over to the dishwashing station. As I run hot water over the glass, the irony hits me. This is where I started at Thistle.

And this is where it will end.

"Come on," says Naomi, "Luis is waiting for us."

We make our way out the door and through the thick snow. Luis is waiting for us with Norah in his truck. Naomi crawls in the back with her sister, and I sit up front.

As we plow through the snow toward the highway, something in the rearview mirror catches my attention. The lights have come back on.

Naomi sees it at the same time.

"The power's back!" she says.

"We have to go back; won't the freezer—"

She shakes her head. "We can't, the security cameras. They'll see us."

"But won't Devon freeze to death in there?"

Naomi pauses, chewing on her lip. "I'll come back in the morning."

"But—"

She places a firm hand on my shoulder. We make eye contact. "I'll come back in the morning, Sadie."

The look in her eyes. I know what she means. I touch the bruise on my face and turn my eyes to the highway.

And I don't look back.

46

NAOMI

"Mrs. Winthrop, let's go over this again," says the police officer sitting across from me in the dining room.

"As I told you before," I say, smoothing the tablecloth in front of me, "I was coming back from a meeting in New York, with Luis. My sous chef. The roads were a disaster. We couldn't make it out here to the farm, so we stopped off at a hotel for the night. I didn't get here until this morning."

"And the blood?" he says with a skeptical look on his face. I swallow, acting as if the words are upsetting for me.

"It was here when I got here."

The inspector looks at me and squints his eyes. I don't know if he can tell if I'm lying or not. But it doesn't matter. I know enough to know that there's no way he can pin it on me without evidence.

It's pretty simple. Devon bumped his head while he was in the freezer. He must have passed out.

A terrible accident.

When Luis and I arrived this morning, the power was

out again. I didn't know what to expect. I used the opportunity while the cameras were down to grab the keys and unlock the freezer. Devon was already dead. I cleaned up the blood on the floor in the kitchen, slipped the keys into his lifeless hands, and closed the door.

I walked around to make sure there was nothing else the police could use against us; then I made the call.

To be fair, Sadie and I had never planned to kill Devon. But when the power came back on last night, I realized fate had dealt me a hand of cards...and I played them.

"Can you come with me, please?" says the police officer. I follow him across the room, stepping around the broken glass on the floor. There are little yellow tents with numbers all over the crime scene.

I take a deep breath and follow the officer to the doorway of the freezer.

"Ma'am, is this your husband?" he asks, pointing to the body on the ground. It's hard for me to see him this way, even after everything he did to me and my sister. His eyes are lifeless, his jaw slack.

I let all the memories, all the pain of losing my sister come to the surface. The tears finally come. And as the curtain closes on my final act as Norah Winthrop, I say my final line.

"Yes, that's my husband. Devon Winthrop."

47

SADIE

Three Months Later

"Thanks, Sally," I say, pulling the piece of sugar cream pie underneath my nose. I'm back at Mike's Diner for the first time in three months. It's been a journey.

I owe Sally a lot more than just a thanks. The night I left the Winthrop estate, Luis drove me to Mike's Diner, where I stayed in the RV that was parked in the back.

Sally was also there.

She always told me that if I ever needed anything, she would be there for me. I've had a lot of people let me down in my life, but surprisingly, Sally actually came through. When the police came to Mike's to speak to me about what had happened to Devon, Sally provided me with an alibi. She told them that I had been here in the RV since before the storm began.

With my testimony and Naomi's, it was enough for them

to close the case. The newswire sent out the message: *Devon Winthrop dies in a tragic accident.*

I push the pie around with my fork. For the first time in the last year, I'm about to meet with my parole officer, Brian, with a completely clear conscience.

I see Brian walking in the door. He looks about the same as the last time I saw him. With one small difference. It looks like he's lost a little weight. Must be a new girlfriend or some diet his wife has put him on.

Brian sits down across from me. "I ordered you some pie." He raises his eyebrows at me. He's never been particularly friendly, but I knew I could butter him up with some pie.

"Thanks," he says. He takes a bite of the pie. "So, how are things?"

"I have a part-time job right now," I say as I cut into my pie. "And a place to live. But I actually went back to school. At a local culinary institute in Portland."

Brian digs into his pie. "Well, as long as you can provide evidence that you're in school, that works for me," he says.

He looks up at me. "By the way, do you know anything about what happened over at the Winthrop estate?"

My stomach twists. I still feel a little uneasy talking about what happened.

At least I know Devon can never hurt me again.

"I have no idea," I say, taking a bite of my own pie. "I was gone before the accident."

I've lost more than a few nights of sleep thinking about how it all happened. It's true, I hated Devon. But I didn't necessarily want to see him dead.

In the end, it was Naomi's choice, not mine. She has to

make her peace with it. And I have to make mine. I burned the evidence of fraud and deleted the photos.

Only the two of us and Luis know what really happened. And we'll take it to our graves.

The whole situation taught me a valuable lesson about honesty. I was never honest with the Winthrops in the first place. I lied on my résumé. I lied about prison.

Now? I've decided it's better to just go into any situation and tell the truth about my past. Not just because it's the right thing to do, even though that feels good. But because telling the truth frees you from the burden of keeping up a lie.

"Well, Sadie," Brian says, finishing his pie, "I have to admit I'm a little surprised you made it this far. You've been on parole for three years now and no issues. I wasn't sure what was going to happen. Especially when you started working over there at Thistle."

"I'm just full of surprises," I say, smiling back at him.

EPILOGUE

NORAH, THE REAL NORAH

Today they've moved me in front of the window. It's raining outside. Although the rain is brief, I can see palm trees surrounding a small lake. The doctor says I'm on a medication that helps my brain heal, which will help me remember. My memories are coming back slowly.

But in the last couple of weeks, a lot of it has come back to me. Some of the memories have been good. And some of the memories...well, not so good.

Naomi has been to visit me here every day. She's been telling me stories. Stories about what happened after the fire. Something about she and Devon starting a new restaurant at the farm that belonged to Devon's family. I believe she said the name was Thistle.

She said there's more that she needs to tell me, but that I wasn't ready to hear it yet.

But out of all the memories that have returned, most are of Devon. After Naomi left, things at the restaurant began to deteriorate. I remember a lot of fights between the two of us.

Devon has always ridden the line between right and wrong. Even when he worked at the law firm, there was an investigation into some of his unethical behavior.

But for me? I was so obsessed with making Pepper a success I was willing to look past all that. But then he did something really stupid. He took money from the wrong people. We were so deep in debt it would take us a decade to climb out.

And the worst part? The restaurant wasn't doing as well as it did in the first year. Which meant we were about ready to go bankrupt.

I did what I had to do.

Unfortunately, it didn't work out so great for me. I don't know if I'll ever cook again. I know they say never burn your bridges.

But I think my go-to saying might be, never burn down your own restaurant.

ABOUT THE AUTHOR

Leah Cupps is a Multiple-Award Winning Author and Entrepreneur. She writes Thriller, Mystery, and Suspense as well as Middle-Grade Mystery Adventure Books.

Leah's novels are fast-paced thrillers that will keep you up at night as you can't wait to see what happens in the next chapter.

Leah lives in Indiana with her husband and three children. When she isn't losing sleep writing her next novel or scaling her next business, she enjoys reading, riding horses, working out, and spending time with her family.

Did you enjoy *One Last Bite*? Please consider leaving a review on Amazon to help other readers discover the book.

Visit Leah Cupps on her website: www.leahcupps.com

ALSO BY LEAH CUPPS

One Last Bite

You Are Not Alone

Made in United States
Orlando, FL
10 August 2024

50182659R00178